編者的話

英語是跨國服務的工具

由於科技發達、交通便利，餐飲業的經營早已開始跨國躍進，再加上目前外匯管制的解除，國人投資海外經營連鎖店，更是勢在必行；而每年湧進台灣的上百萬觀光客，及日益增多的商務旅客，更是餐廳的一筆大富源。為提昇對外國顧客的服務品質，餐館服務人員的英語會話益形重要。因此，必須有一本專門的書籍來協助餐飲服務人員，訓練各種實務英語會話。

餐飲服務業英語會話專書
新餐館英語 —— 留學生到餐館打工必備
出國旅客點菜用餐指南

「**新餐館英語**」的編撰，在提供餐飲服務人員、及欲赴美經營餐館者提昇實務英會能力，也是留學生到餐館打工必備專書，更是出國旅客，及定居海外人士上餐館時的點菜用餐指南。

Part 1 至 Part 3 簡介歐美三餐、點菜、買單付帳與西餐禮儀、及洋酒與菜餚的搭配，是國人到西餐廳赴宴、交際應酬乃至平時解決三餐所不可不知的相關知識，也是餐飲服務人員所應具備的基本常識。

　　Part 4 至 Part 8 是餐館實務英語會話，分別爲接待服務時的應對技巧、專門料理店的應對技巧、用英文處理抱怨、電話訂位·詢問的應對技巧，以及旅館客房服務部的應對技巧。內容廣泛，從詢問餐廳營業時間、電話訂席、點菜時的應對、自助式早餐、美式早餐、推薦招牌菜·開胃酒、介紹專門料理、主廚和顧客的對談、抱怨送錯菜·服務太慢、飲料或食物灑在客人身上……以至買單付款、找錯錢、詢問遺失物品等共六十回。

　　此外，並搜羅各式各樣飲料、菜名、及每日應對常用的單字及短句，供讀者活用。前後蝴蝶頁及內文並附有各式各樣的菜單，俾使讀者熟悉各種菜單之結構方式，對於點菜或服務顧客必然大有助益。

　　審慎的編校是我們一貫的原則，惟仍恐有疏漏之處，尚祈各界先進不吝指正爲荷。

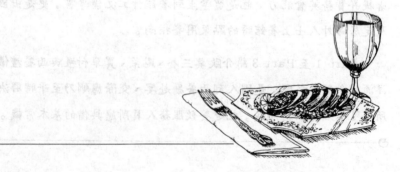

CONTENTS

①

歐美三餐簡介

NO.1

早餐及菜單

　　歐美人非常重視早餐，他們認為早餐若吃得舒服，即表示今天一天會有愉快、滿意的時光。有些人甚至利用早餐時間，邊吃邊談生意。

　　西式早餐一般可分為兩種，一是**美式早餐**（ *American Breakfast*，英國、美國、加拿大、澳洲及紐西蘭等，以英語為母語的國家都屬於此類 ）。一是**歐陸式早餐**（ *Continental Breakfast*，德國、法國等即是 ）。

　　美式早餐內容相當豐富，包括下列五種：

1. 水果或果汁

　　這是早餐的第一道菜，果汁又分為罐頭果汁（ canned juice ）及新鮮果汁（ fresh juice ）兩種。另有一種將乾果加水，用小火煮至湯汁蒸發殆盡，水果豐軟為止，以餐盤端上桌，用湯匙邊刮邊舀著吃。

　　常見的果汁如下：

新鮮果汁

Grapefruit Juice 葡萄柚汁

Tomato Juice 蕃茄汁

Orange Juice 柳橙汁

Pineapple Juice 鳳梨汁

Grape Juice 葡萄汁

Apple Juice 蘋果汁

Guava Juice 蕃石榴汁

Papaya Juice 木瓜汁

V-8 Juice 罐頭綜合菜汁

Fresh Carrot Juice 新鮮胡蘿蔔汁

Mixed Vegetable Juice 什錦蔬菜汁

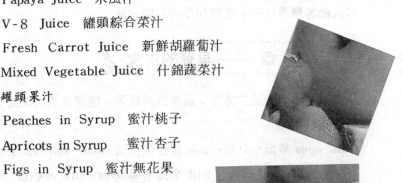

罐頭果汁

Peaches in Syrup 蜜汁桃子

Apricots in Syrup 蜜汁杏子

Figs in Syrup 蜜汁無花果

Pears in Syrup 蜜汁梨子

Loquats in Syrup 蜜汁枇杷

Chilled Fruit Cup 什錦果盅

燉水果乾

Stewed Figs 燉無花果

Stewed Prunes 燉李子

Stewed Peaches 燉桃乾

Stewed Apricots 燉杏乾

2. 穀類 Cereals

玉米、燕麥等製成的穀類食品，如 corn flakes （玉米片），
rice crispies （脆爆米），rye crispies （脆裸麥），puff rice
（泡芙），wheaties （小麥乾），cheerios（保健麥片）等，通
常加砂糖及冰牛奶，有時再加香蕉切片、草莓或葡萄乾等。

此外尚備有麥片粥（ oatmeal ）或玉米粥（ cornmeal ），
以供顧客變換口味，吃時加牛奶和糖調味。

3. 蛋 —— 早餐的主食

這是早餐的第二道菜，通常爲兩個蛋，隨著烹煮方法之不同，
可以分爲：

fried eggs 煎蛋（只煎一面的荷包蛋稱爲 sunny-side up ，兩面煎
半熟叫 over easy ，兩面全熟的叫 over hard 或 over well-
done ）。

boiled eggs 帶殼水煮蛋（煮三分鐘熟的叫 soft boiled ，煮五分
鐘熟的叫 hard boiled ）。

poached eggs 去殼水煮蛋（將蛋去殼，滑進鍋內特製的鐵環中，
在將沸的水中或水面上煮至所要求的熟度。）

scrambled eggs 炒蛋

omelet 蛋捲（也可以拼成 omelette 。）

煎蛋、煮蛋、炒蛋等由客人選擇火腿（ ham ）、醃肉（ bacon ）、
臘腸（ sausage ）作爲配料，以鹽、胡椒（ pepper）調味。bacon

有人要脆的，即 crisp 。蛋捲則有下列各種形式：

Plain Omelet　普通蛋捲

Ham Omelet　火腿蛋捲

Ham & Cheese Omelet　火腿乳酪蛋捲

Spanish Omelet　西班牙式蛋捲

Souffléd Omelet with Strawberries　草莓蛋捲

Jelly Omelet　果醬蛋捲

Cheese Omelet　乳酪蛋捲

Mushroom Omelet　洋菇蛋捲

蛋捲通常用鹽與辣醬油（ tabasco ）調味，而不用胡椒，因為胡椒會使蛋捲硬化，也會留下黑斑。

4. 土司和麵包

吐司通常烤成焦黃狀，要注意 *toast with butter* 和 *buttered toast* 的不同。toast with butter 是指端給客人時，吐司和牛油是分開的。buttered toast 是指把牛油塗在吐司上面之後，再端給客人，美國的 coffee shop 大都提供這種 buttered toast 。

此外，還有下列各種糕餅，以供客人變換口味。注意吃的時候不可用叉子叉，要用手拿，抹上牛油、草莓醬（ strawberry jam ）或橘皮醬（ marmalade ），咬著吃。常見的有：

Corn Bread　玉米麵包

Plain Muffin　鬆餅（須趁熱吃，從中間橫切開，塗上牛油、
　　　　果醬、蜂蜜或糖汁。）

Corn Muffin　玉米鬆餅

English Muffin　英國鬆餅

Biscuit　餅乾

Croissant　牛角麵包（英國人則稱為 crescent roll ）

Waffles　壓花蛋餅（可塗上牛油或楓樹蜜汁，用一隻叉子
　　　　連切帶叉卽可）

Glazed Doughnut　糖衣油煎圈餅（吃油煎圈餅要用手指拿
　　著咬）

Chocolate Doughnut　巧克力油煎圈餅

Jelly Doughnut　果醬油煎圈餅

Plain Doughnut　素油煎圈餅

Powdered Sugar Doughnut　糖粉油煎圈餅

Buckwheat Pancakes　蕎麥煎餅（通常有三片或四片，吃
　　時將牛油放在熱煎餅上使其溶化，然後將楓樹蜜汁塗在
　　上面，用叉子邊割邊叉著吃）

Hot Cakes with Maple Syrup　楓樹蜜汁煎餅

French Toast　法式煎蛋衣麵包片（這是將吐司沾上蛋和
　　牛奶調成的汁液，在平底鍋煎成兩面發黃的吐司，吃時
　　可塗果醬、或鹽及胡椒粉。）

Cinnamon Rolls　肉桂捲子

Miniature Danish Rolls　丹麥小花捲

Hot Danish Rolls　牛油熱烘丹麥花捲

5. 飲料　Beverages

　　指咖啡或茶等不含酒精的飲料。所謂 *white coffee* 是指加奶精（cream）的咖啡，也就是法語中的 *café au lait* ，較不傷胃。不加奶精的咖啡就稱爲 *black coffee* 。

　　在國外，tea（茶）一般是指紅茶而言。如果要綠茶則須指明 green tea 。早餐的咖啡和紅茶都是無限制供應。

　　歐陸式早餐比美式早餐簡單，內容大致相同，但不供應蛋類，客人想點叫蛋類食品時，得另外付費。

美 國 式 早 餐

Orange Juice
柳 橙 汁

Porridge
麥 片

Corn Flakes
玉 米 片

Shredded Wheat
麥 絲 卷

Choice of
隨意選擇

Poached Eggs
去殼水煮蛋

Scrambled Eggs
炒 蛋

Bacon & Eggs
醃 肉 蛋

Ham Omelette
火腿蛋捲

Toast & Butter
烤 吐 司

Marmalade
橘 皮 醬

Strawberry Jam
草 莓

Tea
茶

Coffee
咖 啡

歐 陸 式 早 餐

Fruit Juice
菓 汁

Tea
茶

Coffee
咖 啡

Cocoa
可 可

Croissants
牛角麵包

Brioches
奶油蛋捲

Marmalade
橘 皮 醬

Confiture
果 醬

A La Carte
早餐零點菜單

FRUIT JUICES 果汁類

Apple Juice	蘋果汁
Grape Juice	葡萄汁
Carrot Juice	胡蘿蔔汁
Orange Juice	柳橙汁
Pineapple Juice	鳳梨汁
Guava Juice	蕃石榴汁

COMPOTE OF FRUITS 燉乾果類

Apples	燉蘋果
Pears	燉梨子
Peaches	燉桃子
Prunes	燉乾李

CEREALS 穀類

Porridge	麥片粥
All Bran	麥麩條
Corn Flakes	玉米片
Special K	特別 K
Grapenuts	粒狀麥粉
Puff Wheat	小麥泡芙
Shredded Wheat	麥絲卷
Sugar Corn Pops	糖爆玉米花

BEVERAGES 飲料

Tea	紅茶
Coffee	咖啡
Cocoa	可可
Chocolate	巧克力
Fresh Milk	鮮奶
Yoghourt	酵母乳

EGGS & OMELETTES 蛋類

Boiled Eggs	帶殼水煮蛋
Poached Eggs	去殼水煮蛋
Ham & Eggs	火腿蛋
Bacon & Eggs	醃肉蛋
Plain Omelette	素蛋捲
Scrambled Eggs	炒蛋
Chicken Omelette	雞肉蛋捲
Cheese Omelette	乾酪蛋捲
Tomato Omelette	蕃茄蛋捲
Minced Ham Omelette	碎火腿蛋捲
Kidney & Mushroom Omelette	香菇牛腰蛋捲

FISH 魚類

Kedgeree	印度燴魚飯
Fish Cakes	炸魚餅
Kippered Herring	燻鯡魚
Finnan Haddie & Poached Egg	燻鱈魚水煮蛋

FROM THE GRILL 燒烤類

Breakfast Steak	早餐牛排
Kidney & Bacon	牛腰醃肉
Liver & Tomatoes	牛肝蕃茄
Pork Sausage & Mashed Potatoes	豬肉香腸薯泥

WAFFLE & GRIDDLE CAKES

Cinnamon Waffle	玉桂壓花蛋餅
American Waffle	美式壓花蛋餅
Chocolate Waffle	巧克力壓花蛋餅
Waffle & Fried Eggs	煎蛋壓花蛋餅
Buckwheat Cakes	喬麥餅
Griddle Cakes	煎餅

NO. 2

午餐和晚餐

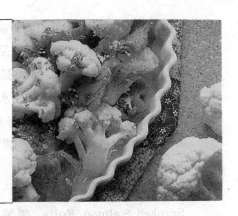

　　午餐和晚餐的菜單相差不多。但是由於午餐食用時間較爲短暫，因而產生了各種商業午餐、快餐，既省時又方便。晚餐則是正餐時間，可以慢慢地品嚐各種美食，通常比較正式，也比較講究，因此男士要穿西裝、打領帶，女士不可穿長褲或短褲，必定要穿洋裝。

　　無論是午餐還是晚餐，菜單（ menu ）上都分爲兩種，一是 *table d'hôte* 稱爲和菜、客飯或定餐，一是 *à la carte* 稱爲點菜式，依菜單零點菜餚。

　　定餐（ table d'hôte ）是由固定的幾種菜餚所組成的，分A餐、B餐、商業快餐等，除了主菜肉類可隨客人點叫外，湯、生菜沙拉、麵包、甜點、飲料等，並沒有選擇的餘地，但價格却很大衆化。

午餐和晚餐通常包括下列五項：

1. 開胃菜 Appetizer

　　正餐前所上之開胃食品，用以促進食慾，有些還附有 *canapé*（塗上乳酪或魚子醬的薄吐司）。常見的開胃菜有：

Shrimp Cocktail　鮮蝦開胃品（用杯子盛放）

Oyster Cocktail　鮮蠔開胃品

Crab Meat Cocktail　蟹肉開胃品

Chilled Fruit Cup　什錦冰水果

Chilled Vegetable Juice　冰鎮蔬菜汁

Assorted Relishes　什錦開胃

Smoked Oyster　煙燻鮮蠔

Smoked Perch　煙燻鱸魚

Smoked Salmon Rolls　煙燻鮭魚捲

Herring in Sour Cream　酸奶油拌鯡魚

Baby Tomato filled with Crab Meat　蟹肉瓤小蕃茄

Strasbourg Pate de Foie Gras　正法國鵝肝醬

Russian Black Caviar　俄國黑魚子醬

American Celery　美國芹菜心

2. 湯 Soup

　　繼開胃菜之後端上來的第二道菜即是湯。一般餐廳供應清湯（clear soup）和濃湯（thick soup）兩種。喝湯的動作是將**湯匙由內向外**，慢慢自碗中將湯舀起。常見的西式羹湯有下列幾種：

Beef Vegetable Soup　菜丁牛肉清湯

Chicken Mushroom Soup　草菇丁濃雞湯

Chili Beans　墨西哥辣豆湯

Green Turtle Soup　水魚清單

Clam Chowder Soup　蛤肉羹（蛤肉加馬鈴薯、洋葱下去燉）

Green Pea Potage　豌豆羹（濃湯）

Chicken Consommé　雞羹（清湯）

Chicken Cream Soup　奶油雞羹湯

French Onion Soup　法式洋葱湯

Oxtail Soup　牛尾湯

Chicken Mushroom Soup　香菇清雞湯

Cream of Mushroom Soup　奶油香菇湯

Cream of Tomato Soup　奶油蕃茄湯

Cream of Corn Soup　奶油玉米湯

Russian Borsch　羅宋湯

Iced Madrilene　冰凍蕃茄芹菜湯

3. 主菜 Entrée

法語叫 " entrée "，美語稱爲 " main dish "，通菜都是肉類及海鮮類。

Veal Sweetbread in Puff Pastry　牛仔核酥批

Pork Chop Cutlet, Robert Sauce　豬排肉片

Veal Cutlet Vienna　維也納小牛肉片

Breaded Lamb Cutlet　羊排肉片

Pheasant in Casserole　原盅焗山雞

Duck a l'orange　鮮橙燴鴨

Beef Goulash　匈牙利燴牛肉

Chicken Kiev　俄式炸鴨

Escalopes Holstein　德式小牛肉

Smoked Pork Chops　燻豬排

Beef Stroganoff　德式炒牛肉絲

Mixed Grill　什錦鐵扒

Chicken à la King　皇家雞飯 (加辣椒醬)

Chicken or Shrimp Curry　咖哩雞或鮮蝦

Calf Liver with Bacon　牛肝燻肉

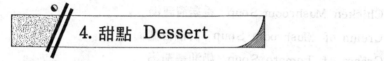

4. 甜點 Dessert

　　包括水果、冰淇淋、布丁、乳酪等。餐後吃點甜的東西，可以調節油膩。

Pineapple Fritters　鳳梨餡油炸餅

Cream Puff　奶油泡芙

Blueberry Pie　藍莓派

Cherry Pie　櫻桃派 (餡餅)

Pecan Pie　核桃派

Lemon Chiffon Pie　檸檬奶油派

Lemon Custard　檸檬軟凍

Mint Sherbet　薄荷雪碧(果汁肉放入牛奶、蛋白等冰凍而成的食物)

Coffee Ice Cream　咖啡冰淇淋

Strawberry Ice Cream　草莓冰淇淋

Chocolate Ice Cream　巧克力冰淇淋

Vanilla Ice Cream　香草冰淇淋

Mango Ice Cream　芒果冰淇淋

Mint Ice Cream　薄荷冰淇淋

Crushed Cherry Ice Cream　櫻桃冰淇淋

Walnut Ice Cream　核桃冰淇淋

Chocolate Sundae　巧克力聖代

Strawberry Sundae 草莓聖代

Banana Split 香蕉船（香蕉上放三種冰淇淋聖代）

Vanilla Cream Cake 香草蛋糕

Swiss Chocolate Ice Cream 瑞士巧克力冰淇淋

Chocolate Malt 麥芽巧克力冰淇淋

Rice Pudding 白米布丁

Custard Pudding 雞蛋牛奶布丁

5. 飲料 Beverages

　　包括咖啡、紅茶、可樂、牛奶、果汁、啤酒等。如果是 *alcoholic beverages* 或 *liquor* 就是指含酒精成分的飲料，像威士忌、白蘭地、琴酒等（酒精成分超過 40 %的烈酒稱爲 *spirits* ）。

Tea 熱茶（紅茶）

Coffee 熱咖啡

Hot Chocolate 熱巧克力

Cocoa 熱可可

Iced Tea 冰紅茶

Iced Coffee 冰咖啡

Orange Juice 柳橙汁

Orangeade 橘子水

Lemonade 檸檬水

Lemon Squash 檸檬果汁

Pepsi（Pepsi Cola）百事可樂

Cherry Coke 櫻桃可樂

Apple Cider 蘋果西打

Sarsaparilla 沙士汽水

Root Beer 麥根汽水

Cream Soda 奶油蘇打

Grape Soda 葡萄蘇打

Yoghourt 酵母乳

Ginger Ale 薑汁汽水

Milk 牛奶

Butter Milk 酸牛奶

Skim Milk 脫脂牛奶

Vanilla Milk Shake 香草奶昔

Vanilla Malt 香草麥芽啤酒

Chocolate Milk Shake

　　巧克力奶昔

咖啡館點叫食物的方式

　　西方的咖啡館（ *coffee shop* 或 *café* ）就相當於台灣的冰果店或麵店，供應冷飲及速簡的三餐，有些是二十四小時營業。

　　早上供應大衆化的早餐，如醃肉、火腿、蛋、吐司、煎餅、牛奶、咖啡等。中午供應快餐、三明治、熱狗、漢堡等，是不帶便當（ lunch box ）的人解決午餐的場所。晚餐供應的牛排、豬排、魚、蝦及雞肉等，價格比大餐廳低廉許多，但不供應酒類。

　　咖啡店的服務生多爲女性（ waitress ），櫃枱後面穿白色制服的冷飲服務生則多爲男性，稱爲 *fountain boy* 或 *soda jerk* 。

　　客人點三明治時，服務生會問，是要用普通的白麵包、裸麥麵包，還是全麥麵包來夾 " *How do you want your sandwich, sir? On white, rye or whole-wheat bread?* " 此外還會問客人吐司要不要烤過 " *Would you like your sandwich plain or toasted?* "

　　如果客人要的是漢堡，服務生會問裏面要不要夾酸黃瓜等調味料和洋蔥 " *Do you want relish and onion on your hamburger?* "

點菜與西餐禮儀

NO. 1
點菜的
技巧與服務

　　點菜大致分定餐和零點兩種方式。

　　定餐（ table d'hôte 也稱為和菜）除去主菜肉類可隨客人喜好點叫外，湯、生菜沙拉、麵包、甜點、咖啡或紅茶都是固定的。

　　如果手拿菜單，卻不知從何處看起，可以問 waiter：

　　　・*What's today's special*？（今天的特餐是什麼？）

　　　・*Do you have anything special on the menu today*？
　　　（今天的菜單有什麼特餐？）

　　　・*What's included in your luncheon special*？
　　　（中午特餐包括些什麼？）

　　如果胃口比較小，或不想點叫定餐，則可以零點（ à la carte ），按菜牌點叫喜歡吃的菜，這時可以向服務生表示 " I'll take the à la carte order. "。

　　先挑選正餐的主菜（ entrée ），主菜必定有馬鈴薯及兩種青菜佐食，如果不喜歡馬鈴薯，可要求換成米飯（ rice ）、麵條（ noodles ）或通心粉（ macaroni ）等。點完主菜以後，再循序點開胃菜、湯、沙拉及拌料、佐餐的酒。

A La Carte

零點菜單

APPETIZERS 開胃小菜

Prawn Cocktail	明蝦開胃品
Shrimp Cocktail	小蝦開胃品
Lobster Cocktail	龍蝦開胃品
Rollmop Herrings	酸鯡魚
Grapefruit Cocktail	葡萄柚開胃品
Chicken Liver Cocktail	雞肝開胃品
Tomato Juice Cocktail	蕃茄汁開胃品
Vegetable Juice Cocktail	蔬菜汁開胃品

SOUPS 湯類

Ox-tail Soup	牛尾湯
Fish Chowder	魚雜膾湯
Tomato Cream	奶油蕃茄湯
Vegetable Soup	什錦蔬菜湯
Russian Borsch	俄式肉湯（羅宋湯）
Asparagus Cream	奶油蘆筍湯
Chicken & Noodle	雞麵清湯
Consomme（hot or cold）	（冷或熱）清湯

EGGS & OMELETTES　蛋類及蛋捲

Ham & Eggs	火腿煎蛋
Bacon & Eggs	鹹肉煎蛋
Poached Eggs & Grilled Ham	去殼水煮蛋火腿
Scrambled Eggs with Chicken Liver	雞肝炒蛋
Cheese Omelette	乾酪蛋捲
Chicken Omelette	雞肉蛋捲
Minced Ham Omelette	火腿蛋捲
Beef & Onion Omelette	牛肉洋葱蛋捲

SEAFOOD　海鮮類

Pomfret Meuniere	牛油煎鯧魚
Frog's leg Fritters	油炸田雞腿
Lobster Thermidor	龍蝦他味多
Fried Prawn Cutlets	炸明蝦肉排
Fried Garoupa Citron	炸石班
Fillet of Sole Florentine	乾酪莧菜龍脷魚
Grilled Sole, Butter Sauce	扒龍脷魚

ENTREES　主菜

Ficcata of Veal	煎牛仔粉仔
Vienna Schnitzel	維也納炸小牛肉排

Chicken à la King　　　　　　　皇家雞飯

Chicken à la Kiev　　　　　　　炸基輔雞

Hungarian Goulash　　　　　　　匈牙利會牛肉

Breaded Pork Chop　　　　　　　粉炸猪排

Spaghetti Bolognaise　　　　　　肉醬粉仔

Breaded Lamb Cutlet　　　　　　粉炸羊排

Cauliflower & Ham au Gratin　　乾酪火腿菜花

Hamburger Steak & Fried Egg　牛排扒煎蛋

FROM THE GRILL　烤扒肉類

Sirloin Steak　　　　　　　　　扒西冷扒

London Broil　　　　　　　　　倫敦什扒

T Bone Steak　　　　　　　　　T 骨牛排

Spring Lamb Chop　　　　　　　扒羊仔排

Stuffed Pork Chop　　　　　　　扒釀猪排

Calf's liver & Bacon　　　　　　扒牛仔肝鹹肉

FROM COLD BUFFET　凍肉類

Game Pie　　　　　　　　　　　凍野味派

Veal & Ham Pie　　　　　　　　牛仔火腿派

Roast leg of Pork　　　　　　　凍烤猪腿

Roast leg of Lamb　　　　　　　凍烤羊腿

Roast Sirloin Beef　　　　　　　凍燒牛肉

Roast　Spring　Chicken　　　　　凍　燒　雞

Roast　Turkey　&　Ham　　　　　凍火雞火腿

Cottage　Cheese　&　Pineapple　　鳳梨鮮乳酪

CURRIES　咖哩類

Fish	咖哩魚	Chicken	咖哩雞
Prawn	咖哩明蝦	Meat Balls	咖哩肉丸
Lobster	咖哩龍蝦	Spring Lamb	咖哩羊肉
Julienne of Beef			咖哩牛肉絲
Egg & Asparagus			咖哩蘆筍蛋

DESSERTS　甜點類

Peach　Melba　　　　　　　　烤脆薄桃片

Sherry　Trifle　　　　　　　　雪莉蛋糕

Orange　Sherbet　　　　　　　柳橙雪碧

Pear　Belle　Helene　　　　　　沙梨希倫

Mixed　Fruit　Salad　　　　　　什錦水果沙拉

Pineapple　Alexandra　　　　　亞歷山大鳳梨

Fruit　Pie　&　Cream　　　　　奶油水果派

Apple　Pie　à　la　Mode　　　　冰淇淋蘋果派

Lemon　Meringue　Pie　　　　　檸檬蛋白糕

Chocolate　Cream　Pie　　　　　巧克力奶油派

有些人怕發胖，故午餐從簡，只叫一客沙拉，再點個湯或脫脂牛奶了事。這時可以這麼表達：

- *I'm on a diet. I just want a soup and crackers.*
  （我在節食，只要一份湯和脆餅乾就好。）

- *I want fruit cake and skimmed milk.*
  （我要水果蛋糕和脫脂牛奶。）

- *Just a fruit salad and buttermilk.*
  （只要一份水果沙拉和酸牛奶。）

在菜單上找不到想要的東西時，只消開口問一聲，服務生就會指給你看。

" Where are your salads ? "（你們的沙拉在哪裡？）

" They are right here on the bottom. "（就在底下這裡。）

有些餐廳或俱樂部每星期會在固定的時間（如每星期二中午或晚上）準備自助餐（ buffet ），以饗顧客。*smorgasbord* 即是一種瑞典式自助餐，供應多種精美的開胃食品。這時服務生也不會忘了告訴客人，以便提供對方更多的選擇機會。

"Why not try our buffet dinner ? The roast beef is excellent."（要不要試試我們的自助餐？碳烤牛肉棒極了。）

自助餐的好處在於經濟實惠，可以自由選擇可口的菜式，而且份量不限，不夠時可以再拿（ come for seconds ）。有的餐廳要憑餐券（ voucher 或 buffet ticket ）拿取，餐券在出納櫃枱（ cashier ）可以買到。有些則不必餐券自由拿取，等餐畢再付帳。

NO. 2
結帳須知
及實用語句

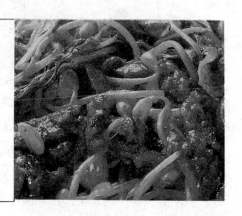

　　吃完飯，餐巾只要順勢放回桌上即可，不用叠得好好的。這時服務生會走上前再添些冰開水，並隨口問問還要不要別的東西 " *Would you care for anything else* ？ " 如果是午飯，通常至此為止，可以回答 " *No，I'm full. Just the bill，please.* " （不，我吃飽了，把帳單給我就好。）但如果是晚間，可能客人會要杯飯後酒繼續坐下去。

　　打算離去時，如果服務生不在跟前，喊一聲 "Waitress，*the check，please.*" 或 " *Please bring me the bill.* " 他就會把帳單遞過來。此外，也可以舉手招來服務生，然後問 " *May I have my check* （bill），*please* ？ " 。

　　服務生代收帳款時，出納員應把收據面向上放在小盤（ tray ）裡，零錢壓在收據上，再由服務生端給客人。通常客人會順手將盤裡的零錢留給服務生當小費。

　　如果客人必須到櫃枱付帳，服務生應把帳單面朝下，扣著放在桌子上，然後說 " *Please pay the cashier as you go out.* " （您出去的時候請到櫃枱付帳。）自己到櫃枱付帳時，習慣上要在餐桌上留下給服務生的小費。

　　如果是旅館的房客、餐廳的會員或常客，可能會要求用簽帳的" I'll sign for it. " " May I sign for it？"除了旅館的房客以外，通常都得請示經理，這時服務生會對客人說 " *I'll get the manager for you. He'd be most glad to help you.* "。

　　客人要用信用卡（ credit card ）簽帳時，服務生必須問清楚是哪一種信用卡。如果是餐廳可以接受的，除了信用卡以外，還要向客人要身份證明 " *May I have your I.D.* (identification card), please?" 以便出納員抄錄或刷印卡片號碼和該家銀行或公司的名字，將來好和他們結帳。

　　如果餐廳不習慣接受信用卡，或與該家銀行、公司無金錢業務往來，只好說聲抱歉了 " I'm sorry. *Our restaurant doesn't accept cards for that company.* "。

　　和美國人一起吃飯，未先講好誰請誰時，不必因為客氣而搶付帳，最好各付一半或各付各的（ go Dutch ）。如果你堅持要付帳，他會認為你想打他的歪主意。

　　但商業人士利用吃飯時間，洽談生意及業務的情況，因有利害關係，常有彼此代付的情形。因此，服務生和出納員要問清楚：

　　"Will these be on a separate bill ？ *"*（要分開算嗎？）

　　" Together or separately ？ *"*（要一起算還是分開來算？）

如果要分開算，則回答 " Make these separate. "如果要一起算，就說 " Put them together.　I'll pay for it. "或 " Put all those on one bill. "。

　　如果你想幫對方付帳，最好事先表示" *I'll treat this time.* "（這回我請客。）或 " *I'll take care of the bill.* "（帳單由我來付。）如果對方的確有誠意想付帳，不可與之拖拖拉拉搶付帳，以免失去君子風度：" All right, if you insist. "（好吧，如果你堅持的話。）

NO. 3
西餐禮儀
及注意事項

　　西方人與中國人的習俗畢竟不同，因此餐桌上的禮儀自然有相當的差異。譬如**喝咖啡**的時候，必定要端起杯子（ cup ）來，**不可用茶匙（ *tea spoon* ）舀著喝**，也不可以用茶匙舀起來嚐甜度或燙度，當然更不可以用嘴吹冷了。如果不熟悉這些基本的禮儀，可能會為自己帶來困窘，或使對方困窘而不自知。

　　用餐禮儀不僅客人應該了解，服務生在掌握服務技巧以前，也必須先學會用餐的禮儀，才能提高服務的品質。

　　東西方皆然的基本餐桌禮儀，如腳不可隨意伸出座位外，以防撓及別人，口中殘渣應用手取下，不可由口吐出等等，此處不再贅述。以下擬提出西餐的刀叉擺置與使用、不同食物的特別注意事項等，供讀者參考。

1. 用刀叉切食物時，應每次切一片或一塊，**不可同時全部切細**。

2. 茶匙不可放入口中，攪拌後應放在茶碟（ saucer ）中，不可留在杯子裏。

3. 湯匙可以入口，但喝完湯以後就放在盤子上，匙柄放在右邊，匙心向上與桌邊平行。

◎ 餐桌佈置圖

1. napkin〔'næpkɪn〕餐巾
2. dinner plate 餐盤
3. soup spoon 湯匙
4. fish knife & fork
   魚刀、魚叉
5. meat knife & fork
   肉刀、肉叉
   a. for fowl 吃雞肉、鳥肉用
   b. for meat 吃牛、豬、羊肉用
6. bread and butter plate
   麵包盤
7. butter knife 奶油刀

8. dessert spoon 甜點茶匙
9. goblet〔'gɑblɪt〕水杯
10. wine glass 葡萄酒杯
    a. red wine 紅葡萄酒
    b. white wine 白葡萄酒
11. sherry glass 雪莉酒杯
12. Champagne glass 香檳酒杯
13. condiments〔'kɑndəmənts〕調味品
14. butter bowl 奶油盅
    (= *butter container*)

4. 正餐中，刀、叉、湯匙等餐具有好幾套，應該 **由最外面的餐具開始，**
按次序向內使用。最大的匙是喝湯的湯匙，最大的刀叉是吃肉用的。

5. 右手持刀，左手持叉，邊切邊食，是英國習慣，美國習慣則切後把
刀子放在盤邊，右手持叉取食。

6.用餐中要喝水或喝酒時，刀叉放置的方式如下：

・**美國式**：將叉橫放在盤子中，柄放在盤的右邊，刀的兩端都放在盤邊上，刀柄在右邊，刀刃向外。

・**英國式**：刀叉柄分靠在盤邊上，而將末端放在盤子上端。

・**歐洲式**：刀叉末端交會於盤心，兩柄分放在桌上，刀在右邊，叉在左邊，和餐桌邊成三角形。

食用中刀叉的擺放位置

(A) 美國式　　　(B) 英國式　　　(C) 歐洲式

（把刀子放在盤子邊緣，就是暗示服務生「我還未吃完」）

食用後刀叉的擺放位置

(A) 美國式　　　(B) 英國式　　　(C) 歐洲式

7.吃完一道菜後，應將用於這道菜的刀叉並排橫放在盤中，刀口向叉。

8.吃蠔肉用的叉，使用完後，放在盤中部的蠔堆上。

9. 正式敬酒是在上香檳酒時。不能喝酒時，應聲明，不可將杯倒置。

10. 餐巾（napkin）應平舖在膝上，不可掛在胸前。大餐巾可以摺爲兩折，小餐巾則完全打開。

11. 如果餐具不愼掉在地上，不要自己彎腰去撿，應請服務生代勞。

此外，要注意吃相雅觀與否。麵包或吐司到底應該用咬的，還是撕成小片後入口，對東方人來說畢竟不容易分清楚。其他各種食物的吃法，也通常有其特定的習慣，最好能事先了解。

1. 每份早餐均附帶兩片烤黃的**吐司**，配以牛油、果醬，吃時要**用咬的**，不可用手撕著吃。不可把蛋夾在吐司上拿著咬，以免蛋黃流得到處都是。

2. **三明治、漢堡或熱狗要用咬的**，用手撕著吃，裏面的雞片、火腿片等會弄得滿手滿地都是。

3. 蛋黃、蛋白要一起邊割邊吃，不可先吃掉蛋白，再將蛋黃一啜而入。蛋黃破了是理所當然的，此時可利用吐司輔助叉子刮起來。

4. 吃麵包、餅干或小粒水果、薯片等，可以用手取食之，但**麵包應撕成小片**，塗牛油或果醬後入口。

5. 吃水果時應切成小塊，並取出核子。

6. 麵包應取自己左手前面的，不可借取。

7. 客人就座後送上來的冰開水，英文就叫 *water*，不可刻意強調 *iced water*。

8. a cup of coffee 是一杯熱咖啡，要冰咖啡必須指明 *iced coffee*。

9. 茶匙（tea spoon）是舀糖及攪拌用的，不可碰嘴。攪畢後不可留在杯子裏，要朝上放在茶碟（*saucer*）右上方。

10.餐桌上喝咖啡，只端杯子茶碟不動。喝完後把杯子放回茶碟的圓圈內。

11.站著或坐在沙發上喝咖啡時，杯子和茶碟要一起拿在手裏，以防灑落。

12.喝飲料時，不可用啤酒或汽水當衆沖洗杯子。

13.西式餐宴人數座位都是固定的，請帖左下角通常印有法文的縮寫 **R.S.V.P.**，意思是「**請答覆**」，故必須肯定答覆是否能夠參加。

14.接受歐美人的餐宴，必須問清楚該穿何種服裝參加，以免與衆不同，貽人笑柄。有些餐廳會規定客人必須穿什麼衣服，否則不准進入。

15.在餐廳，脫下的大衣應寄在存物處（cloakroom），不可放在餐桌上或搭在椅背上。

餐館小常識

❋ on the house 本店奉送；免費

遇到有什麼值得慶祝的事，店老闆有時會大聲呼叫 "Drink any-
thing you want! It's on the house, folks!"（大夥要喝什麼儘
管喝，本店請客。）

❋ Valet Parking 代客停車

開車到高級餐廳，客人不用自己停車，車至入口處，就交給專門的
人代為停車，就叫 valet parking。餐畢結帳後，專員會再把車子開
到門口，小費約一塊美金。

❋ 如何滿足您早餐看報紙的習慣

有些人喜歡邊吃早餐邊看報紙，認為這是一種享受。在大眾化的咖
啡館裏，因為生意太忙，通常不備報紙。但觀光飯店的餐廳為滿足
客人的需要，常有早報供客人索閱。這時你只要向服務生問一聲：
"*May I have the morning paper, please?*" 或 "*Do you have
today's paper?*"，通常都能如願以償。

❋ 提醒客人不要忘了隨身攜帶的東西

常有客人離開時，忘記取走放在桌上或掛在椅背上的雨傘、皮包等，
這時服務生若能開口提醒對方，一定能博得客人的好感，建立餐廳
「服務週到」的形象。

"*Sir, you forgot your umbrella.*"（先生，您忘了拿傘。）

"*Don't forget your purse.*"（別忘了你的錢包。）

"*Are these your things, ma'am?*"

（太太，這些是您的東西嗎？）

3

洋酒與菜餚的搭配

NO. 1
名酒佳餚
相得益彰

　　酒在西餐中是不可或缺的飲料。歐洲各國如義大利、法國、西班牙、葡萄牙等，對酒尤其講究。用餐前有開胃酒（ *apéritif* ），用餐時則佐以葡萄酒，用餐完畢後還有餐後酒，不但正規餐會時如此，就連平常用簡餐時，也有這種習慣。

　　每個國家都有特別的名菜，同樣地各自擁有著名的酒類。尤中以法國最具歷史性，名聞世界的 **Bordeaux**（波爾多葡萄酒）， Cognac （高涅白蘭地酒）， **Burgundy** （布根地葡萄酒），及 Champagne （香檳酒）都產在法國。

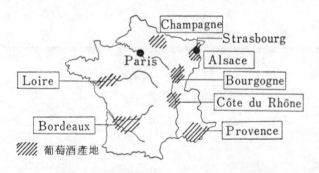

　　Champagne 及 Cognac 都是由於品質優良，而獲得法國政府允許以當地的地名來做商標，香檳邑（ Champagne ）以外所產的發泡葡萄酒，

都只能稱做 *sparkling wine*（法語叫 *vin mousseux*），高涅邑（Cognac）以外所生產的白蘭地則叫做 *eau-de-vie*（生命之水的意思）。

1. 餐前開胃酒

開胃酒（apéritif）又叫餐前酒，通常爲了增進食慾，都飲用一些較爲強烈的辣味酒。**正規的開胃酒以雪莉酒（ *sherry* ）和苦艾酒（ *vermouth* ）最具代表性**，有些人也喜歡以雞尾酒（cocktail）來充當飯前酒。

雞尾酒是用琴酒（gin）、威士忌（whiskey）、蘭姆酒（rum）、伏特加（vodka）等烈酒爲基酒，加冰塊、可樂、蘇打水、果汁、或其他清涼飲料所做成的混合酒，可消暑解渴，適合炎夏飲用。因爲酒性不同不能亂配，選定一種酒後不可更換，否則會頭暈嘔吐。

以下是一些最常見的開胃酒：
Dubonnet　法國紫紅色甜葡萄酒
Dry Vermouth　不甜苦艾酒
Sweet Vermouth　甜苦艾酒
Sandeman-Cream Sherry　奶油紫紅色雪莉酒
Sandeman-Dry Sherry　不甜紫紅色雪莉酒
Sandeman Port　　紫紅色波多酒
Cinzano　苦艾酒和苦橘皮汁調配的酒

2. 佐餐酒

用餐時多半飲用葡萄酒。葡萄酒大致可分爲紅、白和中間色三種，各有其獨特的香味，所以有些料理並不對味，至於如何選擇就要配合所點的菜肴了。一般白葡萄酒通常佐配魚蝦海鮮類，紅葡萄酒和含有辛辣味的白葡萄酒則適宜佐配牛肉、豬肉、雞鴨等肉類食物。中間色的粉紅葡萄酒（rosé）可以佐配任何食物。

以下為料理和酒類搭配的詳細對照表：

Beef 牛肉	Red Burgundy 布根地紅葡萄酒
Cake 蛋糕	Cold sweet wine 冰冷的甜葡萄酒
Chicken 雞肉	
hot 熱食	Red Bordeaux or Burgundy 波爾多或布根地紅酒
cold 冷食	Semi-dry white 稍甜白葡萄酒 Rhine wine 萊茵葡萄酒
Cheese 乾酪	
soft 軟（如Brie, etc）	Red Bordeaux 波爾多紅葡萄酒
firm 硬（如Cheddar ）	Robust red 羅勃斯特紅酒 Burgundy 布根地酒
blue 藍	Port 波多酒（葡萄牙產的甜紅葡萄酒）
Desserts 甜點	Sweet wine 甜葡萄酒 Sauternes 索德尼白葡萄酒 Champagnes 香檳酒
Duck 鴨肉	Côtes-du-Rhône 寇斯杜房葡萄酒
Fish 魚類	Dry white 不甜白葡萄酒 Semi-dry white or rosé 稍甜白或粉紅葡萄酒
Fruit 水果	

apples 蘋果	Red wine 紅葡萄酒
cherries 櫻桃	Rhine wine 萊茵葡萄酒
grapes 葡萄	Sauternes 索德尼白葡萄酒
peaches 桃子 pears 梨子	
strawberries 草莓	Port 波多酒
Game birds 獵鳥	Full-bodied red 濃郁的紅葡萄酒
Ham 火腿	Light white wine 淡的白葡萄酒
Lamb 羊肉	Light Bordeaux wines
	淡的波爾多葡萄酒
Soup 湯	Sherry 雪莉酒
	Madeira　馬第拉白葡萄酒
Shellfish 貝殼類	Dry white 不甜白葡萄酒
	Burgundy 布根地酒
	Rhine wine 萊茵葡萄酒
Turkey 火雞肉	Red Bordeaux 波爾多紅葡萄酒
Veal 小牛肉	Light reds 淡的紅葡萄酒
Venison　鳥獸之肉	Hearty reds　哈第紅葡萄酒
Vegetables 蔬菜	Semi-dry wine 稍甜的葡萄酒
	rosé 粉紅葡萄酒

　　一般而言，紅葡萄酒多半在室溫18°C 左右的溫度下飲用，白葡萄酒和粉紅葡萄酒則必須冰凍後飲用（ 7°C左右 ），味道才會更棒，香檳以冰到 4 至 5°C爲佳，有年代性的波爾多葡萄酒則應保持在21°C 。此外，必須特別注意，不可點叫威士忌或白蘭地等烈性酒佐餐，以免嚐不出食物的美味來。

3. 餐後酒

餐後酒以白蘭地、波多酒（Port）和利口酒（ liqueur ）最具代表性。波多酒多在吃甜點或水果時飲用。利口酒是一種烈性的甜酒，可以清口、幫助消化，喝的時候要一點一滴，慢慢品嚐欣賞它清香的味道。男士們飯後則尤其喜愛啜飲各種香而不甜的名貴白蘭地。

以下為一些最常見的餐後酒：

Martell 馬德爾白蘭地　　　　Hennessy 軒尼詩白蘭地

Courvoisier 可斐斯白蘭地　　Creme de Cacao　可可甜酒

Creme de Banane 香蕉甜酒　Orange Curacao　橙皮甜酒

Creme de Menthe（ green or white ）薄荷甜酒

Cherry Heering 櫻桃白蘭地　Anisette 茴香酒

Cointreau 清甜烈酒　　　　Drambuie 茶色甜烈酒

4. 酒齡的鑑別符號

一般洋酒在酒瓶上都會標上表示貯存年份的符號或縮寫，有時從酒的名字中也可以看出，像 Hennessy X.O.（軒尼詩 X.O.）就表示出酒齡為四十年以上。因此只要熟悉了洋酒中各種年份的代表符號，就不難鑑別出一瓶酒的酒齡了。

酒齡的年份符號和縮寫

Vintage Symbols & Abbreviations

3 年	☆
4 年	☆☆
5 年	☆☆☆
10 - 12 年	V.O.
12 - 17 年	V.S.O.
20 - 25 年	V.S.O.P.
40 年	V.V.S.O.P.
40 年以上	X.O.

在外國餐廳，吃的東西是臨走才算帳的，但喝的酒類則每叫一次就得當場付帳，使用信用卡時則需每次簽名。

當侍者問你要不要邊等邊喝雞尾酒時 " *While waiting, would you like a cocktail*？" 如果你不曉得該點些什麼，則不妨參看同桌的人所點叫的酒，告訴侍者 " *I'll have the same.* "（我也來一樣的），或 " *Make it two.* "（來兩杯）。

此外，常聽人們點酒時提到 dry，如 " *Dry* Martini, please. "（我要不甜的馬丁尼）或 " Manhattan, extra *dry* for me. "（我要完全不甜的曼哈頓酒），dry 的意思就是「不含甜味的」。

NO. 2
洋酒簡介

　　普通葡萄酒的酒精含量是12％－14％（最低含量7％）。酒精含量超過14％以上的飲料，就是烈酒，稱作 *spirits* 或是 *hard liquor*，例如威士忌（whiskey）、琴酒（gin）、蘭姆酒（rum）、雪莉酒（sherry）、伏特加酒（vodka）和白蘭地（brandy）等，都是十分著名的烈酒。西方國家酒類繁多，各有獨特的風味，已經和人民的餐飲生活結合在一起，成為一種西方飲食文化。因此具備一些飲酒的基本常識，不但可以幫助你品嚐洋酒的絕佳風味，同時在舉杯之餘，也可以增加用餐的樂趣！

1. 威士忌 Whiskey

　　威士忌，在蘇格蘭拼作whisky，愛爾蘭和美國人則拼成whiskey。威士忌通常是以玉米和其他穀類作原料，酒精含量約在百分之40～45之間。依照產地的不同，威士忌可以分為Scotch（蘇格蘭）、Bourbon（美國波旁）、Canadian（加拿大）、Irish（愛爾蘭）、British（英格蘭）等。其中較著名的有：

Scotch Whisky 蘇格蘭威士忌

⇨產自蘇格蘭高原，有揮發性的辣味和獨特的蘇格蘭醇香。威士忌需久藏才能飲用，英國政府甚至下令，未滿三年以上的威士忌不得用 Scotch Whisky 的名義出售。

Bourbon Whiskey 波旁威士忌

⇨是一種混合威士忌，用玉米加入裸麥等釀成，再經過著色就是 Bourbon。美國最上等的 Bourbon，牌名叫做 *Jack Daniel's Sour Mash*（傑克‧丹尼爾斯）。

Canadian Whiskey 加拿大威士忌

⇨看起來如冰一般地清澈，喝下去後却無比溫暖。產自加拿大。

目前威士忌酒經常使用多種不同的威士忌互相調和而成，像 Scotch Whiskies 即混合了 20 到 30 種，美國著名的 *Seagram's 7 Crown* 則混合了 75 種。

飲用威士忌時，可以加冰塊、蘇打水和其他飲料。但是**名牌的威士忌最好純酒飲用**，才能品嚐出它與衆不同的醇美滋味。因爲威士忌的酒性較強，容易使喉舌受到刺激，一般都在餐後飲用，才不會影響到對美食菜餚的品嚐享受能力。

淡的威士忌酒，味道停留在舌根的地方；濃的威士忌酒，味道强烈，停留在舌尖和嘴唇上面，有時會令人生厭。**威士忌不能以年代和酒色來分辨好壞**，完全靠飲用時的感受來鑑別。總而言之，「有老式的威士忌，有新式的威士忌，但是沒有壞的威士忌。」

◉ 各種威士忌牌名（brands）：

‧ *Black & White* 黑白威士忌（Scotch）

- *Chivas Regal Scotch*　希娃斯・瑞佳爾（ Scotch ）
- *Grant's*　　　　　　格蘭特威士忌（ Scotch ）
- *J & B*　　　　　　　JB威士忌（ Scotch ）
- *Jack Daniel*　　　　傑克・丹尼爾（ Bourbon ）
- *Jim Beam Whiskey*　金檳威士忌（ Bourbon ）
- *Old Grand-dad Bourbon* 老祖父波旁威士忌（ Bourbon ）
- *Seagrams VO. (5 Star) Whiskey*　西格雷姆VO威士忌（Canadian）

2. 琴酒 Gin

琴酒又稱爲杜松子酒，是用燕麥等穀類或杜松香料爲原料釀成的蒸餾酒。琴酒可以分爲兩種，Dutch Gins（ 荷蘭琴酒 ）和Dry Gin（ 英國、美國琴酒 ）。

Dutch Gins *荷蘭琴酒*

⇨味道濃郁，而且有清新的麥芽香氣，十分特殊，荷蘭是琴酒的著名產地。

Dry Gin *不甜琴酒，產於英國、美國*

⇨無色，味道比荷蘭琴酒淡，但是一樣有種芳香的氣味。英國的 Dry Gin 大部分產在倫敦附近，又稱做 London Dry Gin 。

以琴酒爲基酒，可以調製出千種以上的雞尾酒（ cocktails ），所以有人**稱琴酒爲雞尾酒的心臟**。例如在琴酒中加入微量的苦艾酒（ *vermouth* ），就是一份 Dry Martini （不含甜味的馬丁尼）了。飲用琴酒時，多半攙雜各種不含酒精性的飲料一起喝，喝完後有股輕快飄逸的愉悅感，和一種平靜安適的刺激。

⊙ *各種琴酒牌名*（ brands ）：

- *Gilbey's London Dry*　吉爾伯琴酒（ Dry ）
- *Gordon's Dry Gin*　　高登琴酒（ Dry ）
- *Squire's*　老爺牌琴酒

3. 蘭姆酒 Rum

　　蘭姆酒是利用甘蔗發酵蒸餾製成的，原產自古巴。酒精含量在百分之四十以上，具有特殊的芳香和可口的甜味，主要產自熱帶種植甘蔗的國家，像東、西印度群島，非洲，中南美洲等。蘭姆酒分爲 the very dry（口味較濃郁而且辛辣）和 light-bodied（口味較清淡）兩種口味。

　　蘭姆酒可以拿來直接飲用。但是和琴酒一樣，也是調製雞尾酒的主要基酒，美國大部分都將蘭姆酒用來調製雞尾酒。廚房裡做點心和糖果冰淇淋，也常加入一些蘭姆酒以增加風味。

各種精美的酒籃。
放酒時酒名應朝上，讓客人可以一目瞭然。

⊙ *各種蘭姆酒牌名*（ brands ）：

- *Baccardi*　巴卡底蘭姆酒
- *Lemon Hart Demerara*　檸檬克蘭姆酒
- *Capt. Morgan*　摩根船長（海盜）牌
- *Myer's Planter's Punch Rum*　五味黑蘭姆酒

4. 雪莉酒 Sherry

葡萄牙產製的葡萄酒，中途加上白蘭地（ brandy ）來加強酒性叫做 *Port* （ 波多酒 ），如果是法國的葡萄酒加上白蘭地，那就是 sherry （ 雪莉酒 ）了。雪莉酒的酒精成份含量在百分之十五到十八之間，**開瓶以後，酒質不會變壞**，非常經濟。一般可以分為 Fino 和 Olorosos 兩類。

Fino 菲瑙

⇨顏色淺淡，沒有甜味，味道也比較清淡。

Olorosos 俄羅索

⇨味道較甜，顏色深濃，呈深黃色或者是深棕色，有一股堅果般強烈而濃郁的氣味。

在西餐中，**雪莉酒經常被拿來當作餐前酒**（ apéritif ），增強促進食慾。喝雪莉酒時，可以冰凍過後再飲用，也可以不用冰凍，保持和室內溫度一樣的暖度，都是同樣可口美味，隨各人的喜好而定。但是味道較強烈，酒色呈褐色的Olorosos，因為濃度很高，不適合冰凍，應該在室溫下飲用。

⊙ **各種雪莉酒的牌名**（ brands ）：

- *Sandeman's Five Star*   山地門五星雪莉酒
- *Gilbey's Golden Pale*   吉爾伯金黃雪莉酒
- *Harvey's Bristol Milk*   布烈士桃牛奶雪莉酒
- *Harvey's Bristol Cream*   布烈士桃冰淇淋雪莉酒
- *Primaro Amontillado Sherry*   普里曼羅雪莉酒

5. 伏特加 Vodka

　　伏特加原本產在蘇俄，用小麥或其他穀類蒸製而成。目前世界其他各地也有生產，尤其是美國。酒精含量高達百分之九十五，所以喝伏特加時，必須先加水將酒精稀釋到百分之四十到百分之五十五之間，比較適宜。

　　伏特加的酒色透明，非常純淨，聞起來沒有任何氣味，無香無臭。喝進口中時，也沒有任何酸甜苦辣的味道，只有一股火般的刺激燒上來。因此，除了直接飲用之外，伏特加也拿來調製雞尾酒，是雞尾酒的基酒之一，可以冰凍或是加上冰塊後再喝。

◉ **各種伏特加酒的牌名（ brands ）：**

- ***Smirnoff***　　史敏諾夫皇冠伏特加〔俄；美〕
- ***Wolfschmidt***　　巫爾夫斯密特
- ***Bols***　　保路氏伏特加

6. 白蘭地 Brandy

　　白蘭地是一種蒸餾的葡萄酒，再加上其他果汁酒發酵製成，酒精含量在百分之45 ～ 50之間。幾乎每一個國家都有製造白蘭地酒，但是其中以法國西南Cognac（高涅）一地所生產的白蘭地最著名，是白蘭地酒之王，直接就稱為Cognac酒。

　　上等的白蘭地非常澄淨，純粹。具有一種特殊的美味，而沒有任何刺鼻的香氣，極受飲酒者喜愛。

⊙ 各種白蘭地的牌名（ brands ）：

- *Beehive* 〔V.S.O.P.〕　蜂窩白蘭地
- *Hennessy Napoleon*　軒尼詩拿破崙
- *Hennessy* X.O.　軒尼詩 X.O.
- *Martell 3 Star*　三星瑪特爾白蘭地
- *Ortard Napoleon Cognac*　奧地拿破崙高涅酒
- *Bisquit 3 Star*　三星奎特白蘭地

7. 香檳 Champagne

　　香檳是法國出產的名酒，原產地就在法國東北部的香檳邑一地。由於是利用葡萄酒經過再度發酵所製成的，酒瓶內產生兩次發酵作用，所以在開瓶以後，瓶子裡壓縮的二氧化碳跑出來，爆出巨響，冒出泡沫，帶來一股歡慶喜樂的氣氛，宴會中經常喜歡使用香檳酒來增加熱鬧。

　　香檳是一種高級酒，價錢很昂貴。普通一定得保存四年以上，才能拿來飲用。酒齡在 7 年到 12 年之間的香檳酒，不論是味道，酒色和香氣都達到了頂點，最適宜品嚐。香檳酒可以分為 brut，sec 和 extra sec 三種。

　　brut ⇨ 完全沒有糖份，帶點苦澀味道的上等香檳。

　　sec ⇨ 微帶點甜味的香檳。

　　extra sec ⇨ 不甜的香檳。

　　香檳酒餐前、餐後都可以飲用。尤其是經過長久冰凍後的香檳，味道尤佳，清新明快，喝過後令人有飄飄然的愉悅感。

◉ 各種香檳酒牌名（ brands ）：

- *Lanson Demi Sec*　　蘭珊香檳
- *Pol Roger, Vintage Brut*　　年份保羅渣
- *Pommoroy & Greene Champagne*　　龐麥格林香檳
- *Heidsieck Pink*　　粉紅克錫

8. 苦艾酒 Vermouth

　　苦艾酒又稱法國威末酒，是在白葡萄酒中加入苦艾、香料和其他藥材所製成的。主要產地在法國和義大利。**法國苦艾酒**酒精含量為百分之**19，味道比較辛辣；義大利苦艾酒味道甘甜**，分為紅褐色和金黃色兩種。酒精成分在百分之 15～18 之間，以 Torino Vermouth 最為有名。

　　苦艾酒一般都當作餐前酒，同時也經常用來調製雞尾酒，或者是混合其他飲料一起飲用。

◉ 各種苦艾酒牌名（ brands ）：

- *Dubonnet*　　杜邦納苦艾酒
- *Italian Vermouth, Martini Rossi*　　馬丁尼羅西義大利苦艾酒
- *French Vermouth, Noilly Prat*　　法蘭西苦艾酒

9. 利口酒 Liqueur

　　利口酒是一種餐後甜酒，在英國叫做 cordial 。混合了白蘭地、琴酒、蘭姆酒、威士忌等烈酒，再加上香料和糖漿共同製成。含糖量非常高。

　　利口酒分爲兩種，水果利口酒和植物利口酒。水果利口酒本身具有天然色彩，而植物利口酒則是透明無色，可以用人工方法加上顏色。一般利口酒都很甜蜜，且氣味芬芳，可以調製雞尾酒，或是摻和其他飲料，作爲餐後舒緩鬆懈的飲料。

◉ **各種利口酒牌名（ brands ）：**

- *Anisette*　　安尼榭（茴香利口酒）
- *Cointreau*　　關托（橙味甜酒）
- *Creme de Rosé*　　玫瑰利口酒
- *Creme de Menthe*　　薄荷酒
- *Benedictine D.O.M.*　　法國諾曼地利口酒
- *Apricot Brandy*　　杏仁白蘭地利口酒

10. 雞尾酒 Cocktail

　　雞尾酒是以各種蒸餾酒（ *aquavit* ）爲主，例如琴酒、苦艾酒、白蘭地、威士忌等，然後再加入各種飲料及香料所調製而成的。

　　雞尾酒是一種混合飲料（ *fancy drink* ），最好在調製以後，儘快飲用，否則裡面互相混合的酒精會彼此分離，那麼就嚐不到它獨特的美味了。目前，凡是混合的調味酒都可稱作雞尾酒，總共將近有三千多種。

　　除了宴會中常常飲用雞尾酒之外，一般正餐中，也拿來當作餐前酒。

⊙ 各種雞尾酒牌名（ brands ）：

　・*Bloody Mary*　紅腥瑪麗（摻加胡椒和蕃茄汁）

　・*Manhattan*　紐約・曼哈頓（威士忌中加入甜味的薄荷酒）

　・*Martini*（*BB*）　馬丁尼（琴酒、苦艾酒加上西班牙橄欖,檸檬皮）

　・*Pink Lady*　紅粉佳人（杜松子香料雞蛋酒）

　・*Screw Driver*　螺絲起子酒（伏特加酒混合新鮮橙汁）

開香檳酒的步驟

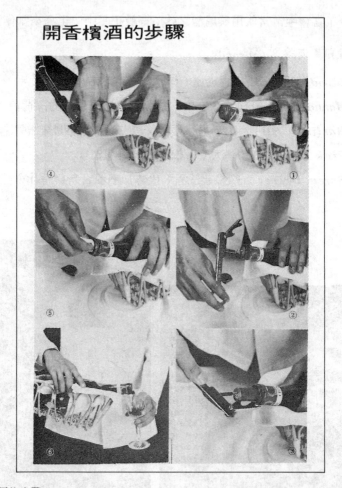

開香檳酒的步驟：

① 把瓶口的鐵絲及錫箔剝掉。

② 以45度的角度拿酒瓶，或放在香檳酒籃上，把開瓶器插入軟木塞，再稍加旋轉。

③ 拔出軟木塞。

④ 拇指壓緊軟木塞並將酒瓶扭轉一下使軟木塞鬆開。

⑤ 俟瓶內的氣壓彈出軟木塞後繼續壓緊軟木塞，並繼續保持45度的角度拿酒瓶，以防止酒從酒瓶冲出。

⑥ 倒酒要分二次，先倒1/3，俟氣泡消失後再度倒滿2/3。

調酒的基本方法

基本酒杯種類

1. Whiskey 〔'hwɪskɪ〕威士忌酒杯
2. Tumbler 〔'tʌmblə〕平底玻璃杯
3. Old-fashioned 〔'old'fæʃənd〕老式酒杯
4. Liqueur 〔lɪ'kjʊr〕利口酒杯
5. Fizz 〔fɪz〕有泡沫的飲料
6. Sherry 〔'ʃɛrɪ〕雪莉酒杯
7. Wine 〔waɪn〕葡萄酒杯
8. Cocktail 〔'kɑk,tel〕雞尾酒杯
9. Cocktail 雞尾酒杯
10. Champagne 〔ʃæm'pen〕香檳酒杯
11. Stein 〔staɪn〕啤酒壺
12. Sour 〔saʊr〕掺有檸檬汁的威士忌酒杯
13. Brandy 〔'brændɪ〕白蘭地酒杯
14. Pilsener 〔'pɪlzənə〕淡黃色啤酒杯

招待服務時的應對技巧

Conversation while Serving the Guest

Please wait to be seated.
請等候（領檯）引導至貴席

　　從餐廳門口帶領客人至座席的叫 hostess（女領枱），有些餐廳是由身穿黑禮服的領班（ head waiter 或 captain ）引導客人入座。

　　引導入座時，應詢問客人之人數 "*How many people, please?*"，及是否有訂位 "*Do you have a reservation?*"。此外，應注意客人的身份及用餐的動機。例如：獨身的男客或女客，應引向靠窗的位置。多位同來的男士，其用餐目的可能是商務上的應酬，應引向角落，讓他們方便談話，不致打擾鄰桌客人。

　　若餐廳客滿，客人必須共用餐桌時，應該事先徵得雙方的同意，問一聲 "*Would you mind sharing a table?*"。如果不得已必須讓客人等候時，可以說明情況 "*I'm afraid all our tables are taken. Would you mind waiting?*" 以求其諒解，並且言明一有空位就馬上通知他，以免客人覺得被忽視了。

　　通知在一旁等候的客人入座時，基本的禮貌絕不可少 "*I'm sorry to have kept you waiting.*" 或 "*We're very sorry for the delay.*"。這樣，縱然對方已經等得不耐煩了，也會受到安撫而平和地坐下來享受他的美食。

引導來賓入席

Showing
the Guest to the Table

Dialogue: *HW*＝**Head Waiter**（服務生的）領班　*G*＝**Guest** 客人

HW : Good afternoon, sir. Welcome to *the Chalet Swiss Restaurant.* 先生，午安。歡迎光臨瑞華餐廳。

G : Thanks. 謝謝。

HW : *How many persons, please?*
　　　請問有幾位？

G : A table for four, please. 四位。

HW : Where would you prefer to sit?
　　　您喜歡哪個位置？

G : Well, by the window, please.
　　　嗯，請給我靠窗的座位。

HW : *I'll show you to your table.* This way, please.
　　　我帶您入坐，這邊請。
　　　Is this fine? 這個位子好嗎？

G : O.K. That'll do fine. 好。這裡很好。

HW： Please take a seat, sir. 先生，請坐。

　G： Thanks. 謝謝。

HW： *A waiter will come to take your order.*　Just a moment, please.

　　　服務生會來侍候您點菜，請稍等。

活用例句精華

① How many persons are there *in your party*, sir？

① 先生，總共有幾位？

② Do you have a *meal voucher*？
（ *breakfast / luncheon /dinner voucher* ）

② 您有沒有餐券？
（早餐/午餐/晚餐餐券）

③ I'll show you to your new table.

③ 我帶您到另一桌去。

④ I'm afraid that area is *under preparation*.

④ 那個地方恐怕還沒準備好。

⑤ I'm afraid that table is reserved.

⑤ 那桌恐怕被訂走了。

⑥ I'm afraid we cannot seat you at the same table. *Would you mind* sitting separately？

⑥ 恐怕沒辦法讓你們坐同桌，你們介不介意分開坐呢？

⑦ Would you like *a high chair for* your son / daughter / child？

⑦ 要不要給您的兒子 / 女兒 / 小孩一張高椅？

⑧ Is anyone *joining* you, sir？

⑧ 先生，還有沒有人要來？

⑨ Would you mind *sharing a table*？

⑨ 您介不介意和別人同桌？

⑩ Another guest wishes to join this table.

⑩ 另一位客人想和您同桌。

⑪ Some other guests wish to join this table.

⑪ 別的客人想跟您共用這張桌子。

⑫ Excuse me, sir. Would you mind *moving over a little*?

⑫ 先生，對不起。您介不介意移過去一點兒？

⑬ Could you *move along one seat*, please?
Another guest wishes to sit at the bar.

⑬ 請移過去一個位子好嗎？
另一位客人想坐在吧枱邊。

⑭ Excuse me, ma'am, but may I pass?

⑭ 女士，對不起，請借過好嗎？

⑮ Could you move your chair closer to the table, please?

⑮ 請把椅子拉近桌邊好嗎？

---

restaurant〔'rɛstərənt〕*n.* 飯店；餐館
prefer to ～ 較喜歡～
take a seat = *be seated* "坐下"
order〔'ɔrdə〕*n.* 點菜；一客 (飯菜)
voucher〔'vautʃə〕*n.* 憑單；收據
luncheon〔'lʌntʃən〕*n.* 午餐 (正式用語)
separately〔'sɛpərɪtlɪ〕*adv.* 分開地
daughter〔'dɔtə〕*n.* 女兒　　share〔ʃɛr〕*v.* 共有；分享
bar〔bɑr〕*n.* 酒吧；酒吧的櫃枱

自助式早餐的入席應對

Buffet-Style Breakfast

Dialogue： *W* = **Waiter** 服務生   *G* = **Guest** 客人

W： Good morning, sir. *A table for two*?
    先生，早安。兩位嗎？

G： That's right. 是的。

W： I'll show you to your table. This way, please.
    我帶您入座，這邊請。
    Please take a seat. *Which would you prefer,*
    tea or coffee?
    請坐。您要茶還是咖啡？

G： Coffee, please. 咖啡。

W： Two coffees? 兩位都咖啡嗎？

G： Yes. 是的。

W： Certainly, sir. *Will there be anything else*?
    好的，先生。還要不要別的？

G： No, that's all, thanks. 不了，謝謝。

W： Thank you, sir. 先生，謝謝。

活用例句精華

① We have both *buffet-style* and *à la carte* dishes. Which would you prefer?

① 我們有自助式和點菜式。您喜歡哪一種？

② Please sit where you like.

② 請隨便坐。

③ The buffet is over there. *Please help yourself*.

③ 自助餐在那邊，請自己動手。

④ The fresh milk is over there *beside the juice machine*.

④ 鮮奶在那兒，就在果汁機旁邊。

⑤ Could you pay *after your meal*, sir?

⑤ 先生，請用餐後再付錢好嗎？

---

buffet〔pʊˈfe〕*n.* 自助餐

buffet-style 是由客人從放置各式各樣食物的自助餐桌上，
　　自己動手拿盤，挑選自己所喜愛的東西，而後自己端至
　　餐桌上食用的方式。

prefer〔prɪˈfɝ〕*v.* 較喜歡

certainly〔ˈsɝtn̩lɪ〕*adv.* 當然

à la carte〔ˌɑləˈkɑrt〕照菜單自行點菜

over there "在那裡"　　*help oneself* "自取(所需)"

juice machine 果汁機　　meal〔mil〕*n.* 一餐

要求客人稍等一會兒

Asking a Guest to Wait

Dialogue : *W =* **Waiter** 服務生　　　*G =* **Guest** 客人

W : Good morning, sir. Welcome to the Le Romantique French Restaurant.

先生，早安。歡迎光臨羅漫蒂法國餐廳。

G : Good morning. 早。

W : How many persons, please?

請問有幾位？

G : *A table for three*, please. 三位。

W : I'm afraid *all our tables are taken*, sir. Would you mind waiting until one is free?

先生，恐怕所有的位子都坐滿了。您介意等到有空位嗎？

G : Well, how long will it take?

要等多久？

W : I'm not sure, sir. *If you are in a hurry*, we also serve
breakfast at the Coffee Shop on the Lobby Floor.
我不確定。如果您趕時間的話，我們在大廳那一樓的咖啡廳也
有早餐供應。

G : That's too much trouble. I'll wait.
那太麻煩了，我還是等一會兒。

W : May I have your name, please?
請問貴姓?

G : Yes, it's Anderson. 安德生。

W : Mr. Anderson. Thank you. Could you take a seat over
there and *I will call you when a table is free*.
謝謝您，安德生先生。要不要到那邊坐，有空位時我再叫您。

G : Fine. Please don't forget!
好的。請別忘了!

W : I won't, sir. （ *a table becomes vacant* ）
先生，不會的。（有一張空桌時）

W : We have a table for you now, sir. This way, please.
We're very sorry for the delay.
先生，現在有位子了，這邊請。非常抱歉耽擱您的時間。

G : Fine. 沒關係。

活用例句精華

① *We can seat you very soon.*

① 我們會很快安排您入座。

② Could you wait about 5 minutes, please?

② 請等五分鐘左右好嗎？

③ Could you wait a little longer, please?

③ 請多等一會兒好嗎？

④ Could you *wait in line* until a table is free, please?

④ 請排隊等到有空位好嗎？

⑤ I'm very sorry *to have kept you waiting*, sir.

⑤ 先生，抱歉讓您久等了。

⑥ An escort will show you to your table. Just a moment, please.

⑥ 侍者會帶您入座，請稍等。

⑦ *Would you prefer a table near the window* (*by the stage, in the center, over there, over here*)?

⑦ 您喜歡靠窗（舞台旁邊，在中間，在那邊，在這邊）的那一桌嗎？

⑧ Would you prefer to sit at a table or at the bar?

⑧ 您喜歡坐餐桌，還是吧枱？

⑨ Would you prefer a table in the main restaurant or in a private room?

⑨ 您喜歡大廳的座位，還是小房間的座位？

⑩ I'm afraid ***this table is reserved for*** 8 ***p.m.***

⑩ 這一桌恐怕有人訂了，晚上八點要來。

⑪ We can seat 3 of you right away but ***if all your party would prefer to sit together***, it will take about 15 minutes.

⑪ 我們可以馬上安排三個座位給你們，但是如果你們要坐在一起，大約要等十五分鐘。

in a hurry "匆忙"　　lobby〔'lɑbɪ〕*n.* 大廳
vacant〔'vekənt〕*adj.* 空的
delay〔dɪ'le〕*n.* 耽擱　　***in line*** 排隊
wait in line（美式說法）＝ queue here（英式）
escort〔'ɛskɔrt〕*n.* 侍者
stage〔stedʒ〕*n.* 舞台
center〔'sɛntɚ〕*n.* 中央；中心
private〔'praɪvɪt〕*adj.* 私人的

必須先預約的餐廳

A Restaurant for Which Reservations Are Necessary

Dialogue : *HW* = **Head Waiter** （服務生的）領班　　*G* = **Guest** 客人

HW : Good evening, ma'am. Welcome to the Gourmet Restaurant. 太太，晚安。歡迎光臨信林餐廳。

G : Thank you. 謝謝。

HW : ***Do you have a reservation***, ma'am？
　　　　太太，您有沒有預約？

G : Yes. 有。

HW : May I have your name, please？
　　　　請問貴姓？

G : Yes, it's Mrs. Broder. 布魯德太太。

HW : Mrs. Broder. *We were expecting you*. This way please. Will this table be fine？
　　　　布魯德太太，我們正在恭候您的大駕。這邊請。這一桌好嗎？

G : Oh, ***this is just fine***. 哦，不錯。

HW : Please take a seat, ma'am. 太太，請坐。

W : Good evening, Mrs. Broder.
晚安，布魯德太太。

G : Good evening. 晚安。

W : *Would you care for an apéritif*?
您要不要來一份開胃酒？

活用例句精華

① We're very happy to see you again.

① 很高興再見到您。

② *Welcome back*, sir.

② 先生，歡迎再次光臨。

③ I'm afraid *that table is reserved*, sir.

③ 先生，那一桌恐怕有人訂了。

④ I'm afraid the table you reserved is not yet ready. Would you mind *waiting until it is free* or *would you prefer another table*?

④ 您預訂的席位恐怕還沒準備好，要不要等它空出來，或者您想坐另一桌？

⑤ I'm afraid that we let another guest sit at your table *since you did not arrive at the reserved time*. Would you mind waiting as the restaurant is full?

⑤ 抱歉，因為您沒有照預約時間前來，所以我們將座位安排給另一位客人了。因為餐廳客滿，您介不介意等一下？

⑥ I'm afraid we require our guests to wear a jacket and tie. We can lend you one.

⑥ 抱歉，我們要求客人要穿外衣打領帶，我們可以借您。

reservation〔,rɛzəˈveʃən〕n. 預約

gourmet〔ˈgʊrme〕n. 能品評及精選美酒美食的人

expect〔ɪkˈspɛkt〕v. 期望

apéritif〔ɑperiˈtif〕n. 開胃酒

reserve〔rɪˈzɝv〕v. 預定 (旅館、座位等)

since〔sɪns〕conj. 旣然；因爲

arrive〔əˈraɪv〕v. 到達

require〔rɪˈkwaɪr〕v. 需要

jacket〔ˈdʒækɪt〕n. 短外衣；夾克

早餐服務之點叫術語

　　一般西餐廳所供應的早餐不外美式早餐（ American Breakfast ），或歐陸式早餐（ Continental Breakfast ），此外也可以由客人依喜好點叫（ *à la carte* ）。

　　在接受客人點菜時，最好一見面就說聲 " Good morning. " 這是應有的禮節。然後奉上菜單，**先遞給女士，無女性時先給長輩**。

　　點早餐所用的英語有限，但是有很多細節必須注意。要問客人想點煎蛋、炒蛋或煮蛋時，應該問 " *How would you like your eggs?* "。如果客人要的是煎蛋，那麼還要問清楚是只煎一面（ sunny-side up ），還是兩面都煎（ over-easy 或 over-hard），這時要用 " *How would you like us to cook your eggs?* "。

　　如果要的是煮蛋，因為有煮三分鐘熟的（ soft boiled ）及煮五分鐘熟的（ hard boiled ）兩種區別，因此要問清楚 " *How many minutes shall we boil your eggs?* "。

　　除此之外，要客人選擇茶或咖啡時，可以說 " Which would you prefer, tea or coffee? "。請問他喝哪一種果汁時，則說 " Which kind of juice would you prefer? "。

美式早餐的服務

American-Style
Breakfast

Dialogue : *W* = **Waiter** 服務生　　　*G* = **Guest** 客人

W : Good morning, ma'am. *Here is your menu.* Could you call
a waiter when you are ready to order ?
太太，您早。這是菜單，決定好要點菜時，麻煩招呼一下服務
生好嗎？

W : *May I take your order now* ?
要點什麼菜？

G : Yes. I'd like an American Breakfast.
我要一份美式早餐。

W : An American Breakfast. Certainly, ma'am. Which kind of
juice would you prefer, grapefruit or orange ?
一份美式早餐。好的，太太。請問您要哪一種果汁，葡萄柚還
是柳丁汁？

G : Grapefruit juice, please.
請給我葡萄柚汁。

W : *How would you like your eggs*?
　　您要什麼樣的蛋？

G : I'd like them fried.
　　我要煎蛋。

W : How would you like us to cook your eggs?
　　您要我們怎麼養？

G : *Over-easy*.　兩面煎黃的嫩荷包蛋。

W : *We serve ham or bacon with your eggs*. Which would you
　　prefer?
　　我們提供火腿或醃肉夾蛋，您要哪一種？

G : Bacon and make it very crisp, please.
　　請給我脆醃肉。

W : Would you prefer *toast* or *rolls*?
　　請問您要吐司還是小圓麵包？

G : Rolls, please.　請給我小圓麵包。

W : *And tea or coffee*?　喝茶還是咖啡？

G : Coffee, please.　請給我咖啡。

W : Now or later?　現在要還是待會兒要？

G : Now, please.　請現在給我。

W : Certainly, ma'am. An American Breakfast *with* grapefruit
　　juice, *fried eggs over-easy*, very crisp bacon, rolls and
　　coffee. Will there be anything else?
　　好的，太太。一份美式早餐、葡萄柚汁、兩面煎黃的嫩荷包蛋
　　、脆醃肉、小圓麵包和咖啡。還要不要別的？

G : No, *that's all*.　不，那樣就夠了。

W： Just a moment, please.
請稍等一會兒。

W： *Thank you for waiting*, ma'am. Please enjoy your
breakfast. 太太，讓您久等了。請享用您的早餐。

活用例句精華

① How many minutes shall we boil
your eggs?

① 您點的蛋要煑幾分鐘？

② Would you like your eggs *sunny-
side up*?

② 您要一面煎黃的荷包蛋
嗎？

③ You may use this *voucher* for an
American Breakfast.

③ 您可以用這張餐券點美
式早餐。

④ I'm afraid that *your order of
eggs is not covered by this
voucher*. Could you pay for them
separately, please?

④ 您點的蛋恐怕不包括在
餐券內，請分開付錢好
嗎？

⑤ Would you *like to care for* some
more coffee, sir?

⑤ 先生，還要不要再來些
咖啡？

⑥ I'll bring an English newspaper
immediately.

⑥ 我馬上帶一份英文報紙
過來。

⑦ I'm afraid all our English news-
papers are being read now. *We
will bring you one* when one
is available.

⑦ 抱歉，恐怕我們的英文
報紙都有人在看。當它
還回來的時候，我會帶
給你一份。

⑧ Excuse me, *may I take your plate*, sir ?

⑧ 對不起，先生，我可以收盤子嗎？

⑨ There is a vending machine outside the restaurant entrance to the left.

⑨ 餐廳外面大門左邊有一部自動販賣機。

---

menu〔'mɛnju〕*n.* 菜單

breakfast〔'brɛkfəst〕*n.* 早餐

grapefruit〔'grep,frut〕*n.* 葡萄柚

orange〔'ɔrɪndʒ〕*n.* 柳丁

over-easy 兩面煎黃的嫩荷包蛋

〔說明〕over-hard 兩面煎黃的老荷包蛋；sunny side-up 一面煎黃的荷包蛋；scrambled eggs 炒蛋。

bacon〔'bekən〕*n.* 醃薰的豬肉

crisp〔krɪsp〕*adj.* 脆的

toast〔tost〕*n.* 吐司；烤麵包片

voucher〔'vautʃɚ〕*n.* 收據；憑單

separately〔'sɛpərɪtlɪ〕*adv.* 分開地；單獨地

immediately〔ɪ'midɪɪtlɪ〕*adv.* 馬上；立刻

available〔ə'veləbl〕*adj.* 可用的

plate〔plet〕*n.* 盤子

vending machine 自動販賣機

entrance〔'ɛntrəns〕*n.* 門口

點菜時的服務
Taking an
A La Carte Order

Dialogue : *W* = **Waiter** 服務生　　　*G* = **Guest** 客人

W : Good morning ma'am. Welcome to the Charming Garden
Restaurant. 太太您早，歡迎光臨湘園餐館。

G : Thank you. 謝謝。

W : May I show you our breakfast menu? *Please take your
time*. 您要不要看早點的菜單？請慢慢看。

G : Ah, thank you. 啊，謝謝你。

W : May I take your order now?
要點什麼菜？

G : Yes, I'll have *a pineapple juice*, a boiled egg with toast
and tea, please.
是的，我要鳳梨汁、煮蛋、吐司和茶。

W : How would you like your eggs, ma'am.
太太，您點的蛋要怎樣煮法？

G : Hard-boiled, please. 請煮全熟。

W：*And your toast, ma'am, light or dark*？
　　您的吐司要稍微烤一下，還是烤焦？

G：Light, please. 請稍微烤一下。

W：Would you prefer your tea with lemon or with milk？
　　您的茶要加檸檬還是牛奶？

G：With milk. 加牛奶。

W：*Now or later*？ 現在要還是待會兒要？

G：*Later will do*. 待會兒就可以了。

W：Will there be anything else？
　　還要不要點別的東西？

G：No, that's all, thanks.
　　不了，那些就夠了。

W：One pineapple juice, one hard-boiled egg *with* toast and
　　tea *to follow*.
　　一杯鳳梨汁、一份羹熟的蛋，再加上吐司和茶。

G：That's right. 對的。

W：Just a moment, please.
　　請稍待。

活用例句精華

① I'm afraid it is not on our breakfast menu.

② The French toast will take about 15 minutes to make. Would you mind waiting?

③ We can serve pancakes very quickly.

① 我們早上的菜單恐怕沒有這項。

② 法國吐司大概要十五分鐘才能做好，您願意等嗎？

③ 我們的薄煎餅可以很快供應。

Charming Garden Restaurant 湘園餐廳
take one's time "不慌不忙"
pineapple 〔'paɪn,æpl̩〕 *n.* 鳳梨
hard-boiled 煮全熟的　　lemon〔'lɛmən〕*n.* 檸檬
follow〔'falo〕*v.* 跟隨
moment〔'momənt〕*n.* 片刻；瞬間
pancake〔'pæn,kek〕*n.* 薄煎餅

接受點菜和推薦料理

在點菜時，客人往往會詢問各種菜式的內容、料理的調製方法等問題。所以，服務生平時要多多充實這方面的知識，熟記有關菜肴的英文說法。

拿菜單給客人點菜時，要給他充裕的時間慢慢選擇 " *Please take your time* " 不要急著問 " *May I take your order?* " （要點什麼菜？）。問客人牛排要幾分熟的術語是 " *How would you like your steak?* " 請問客人要哪一種沙拉佐料時，可以說 " *What kind of dressing would you prefer?* " 。客人點完菜之後，為了確定無誤，最好將所點的菜名重覆唸一遍。

由於餐廳的菜式多，客人難以下決定，服務生要主動向他推薦招牌菜，以充滿信心的態度說明所推薦的菜式內容，這樣可以提高客人對餐廳的信賴程度。飯後可以推薦水果、甜點等食品，晚飯時可視情形推薦酒類。推薦的基本句型是：

①*How about* ＋ 菜名或酒名？

②*I recommend* ＋菜名或酒名。

如果某道菜得花費較長的時間做準備，一定要事先說清楚 "I am afraid *the gratin will take some time to prepare*." ，並且問明對方介不介意，否則得罪了趕時間的客人，倒霉的是自己。

7

受理點菜・推薦食物
Taking the Order
and Recommending Dishes

Dialogue : *W* = **Waiter** 服務生　　*G* = **Guest** 客人

W : Good afternoon, sir. Welcome to the Coffee Shop. May I show you our lunch menu?

先生，午安。歡迎光臨咖啡廳。您要午餐的菜單嗎？

G : Thanks. 謝謝。

W : *Please take your time.*

請慢慢看。

May I take your order, now?

要點什麼菜？

G : Yes, I'll have *a mixed Salad* and *a Sirloin Steak. Which vegetables come with the steak*?

我要一份綜合沙拉和一客沙朗牛排。牛排的副菜是什麼呢？

W : French fried potatoes, carrots and peas.

有炸薯條、胡蘿蔔以及青豌豆。

G : That'll be fine.

不錯。

W : Would you like anything to drink, sir ?
先生，要不要來點飲料？

G : Yes, I'll have some beer *with coffee to follow*.
好的，我要啤酒，再來點兒咖啡。

W : *How would you like your steak*, sir ?
先生，您的牛排要幾分熟？

G : I'll have it *medium rare*, please.
請給我三、四分熟的。

W : Which kind of salad dressing would you prefer, French, Thousand Island or Oil and Vinegar ?
請問您要哪一種沙拉佐料？法式、千島或油醋佐料呢？

G : Do you have any Blue Cheese dressing ?
你們有藍乳酪佐料嗎？

W : I'm afraid not but *I would recommend the French dressing*.
恐怕沒有，不過我推薦法式佐料。

G : I see. O.K. I'll take that.
好吧。我就用那種。

W : Would you like your coffee now or later ?
咖啡要現在喝還是等會兒再喝？

G : Later, please.　等會兒再喝。

W : A medium-rare Sirloin Steak, a mixed Salad, a glass of beer and a cup of coffee. *Will there be anything else* ?
一份三、四分熟的沙朗牛排，一份綜合沙拉，一杯啤酒和一杯咖啡。還要點別的嗎？

G：No , that's all , thanks .
　　不 , 就這些了 , 謝謝 。

W：Thank you, sir. Just a moment, please.
　　謝謝您 , 先生 。請稍等一會兒 。

活用例句精華

①*Are you ready to order now*, sir ?
　① 先生 , 您要點什麼菜 ?

② Could you repeat the order, please ?
　② 請重複一次您點的菜 , 好嗎 ?

③*Which brand of beer*（*cigarettes, whisky*）*would you prefer* ?
　③ 您喜歡哪一種牌子的啤酒（香煙 , 威士忌）?

④ Would you prefer Taiwan or imported beer ?
　④ 您喜歡台灣啤酒或是進口啤酒 ?

⑤ Would you like to see our cake selection ?（*dessert wagon, wine list, cheese board*）
　⑤ 您要看我們蛋糕的種類嗎 ?（甜點車 , 酒牌 , 乳酪櫃）

⑥ May I have your order, sir ?
　 What would you like to order, sir ?
　⑥ 先生 , 您要點什麼菜 ?

⑦ I'm afraid it is not *in season*, sir.
　 I'm afraid it has been *sold out*.
　 I'm afraid it is not on the menu.
　 I'm afraid it must be ordered a day *in advance*.
　⑦ 這種恐怕還未上市 , 先生 。
　　這種恐怕已經賣完了 。
　　這種恐怕不在菜單上 。
　　這種恐怕必須在一天前預約 。

⑧ Which flavour would you prefer, A or B?

⑧ 您喜歡哪一種口味，A 或B？

⑨ Would you like separate checks, sir?

⑨ 先生，你們要分開算帳嗎？

---

recommend 〔͵rɛkə'mɛnd〕 *vt.* 介紹；推薦

mix 〔mɪks〕 *v.* 混合

salad 〔'sæləd〕 *n.* 沙拉；生菜食品

sirloin 〔'sɝlɔɪn〕 *n.* 最好的牛腰肉

vegetable 〔'vɛdʒətəbḷ〕 *n.* 蔬菜

potato 〔pə'teto〕 *n.* 馬鈴薯

carrot 〔'kærət〕 *n.* 胡蘿蔔

medium rare 三、四分熟

〔說明〕 rare 爲未完全煮熟的，medium 約五分熟，well-done 則是全熟。

salad dressing 沙拉佐料

vinegar 〔'vɪnɪgɚ〕 *n.* 醋

cheese 〔tʃiz〕 *n.* 乳酪

recommend 〔͵rɛkə'mɛnd〕 *v.* 推薦

brand 〔brænd〕 *n.* 牌子　cigarette 〔͵sɪgə'rɛt〕 *n.* 香煙

whisky 〔'hwɪskɪ〕 *n.* 威士忌

imported 〔ɪm'portɪd〕 *adj.* 進口的

selection 〔sə'lɛkʃən〕 *n.* 供選擇之物

dessert 〔dɪ'zɝt〕 *n.* 餐後甜點

wagon 〔'wægən〕 *n.* 四輪貨運馬（牛）車

in season " 上市；當令合宜的時間 "

sell out " 賣完 "　　*in advance* " 預先 "

separate 〔'sɛpə͵ret〕 *adj.* 分開的　　check 〔tʃɛk〕 *n.* 帳單

沙拉簡介

　　在中國餐館，正餐開始前有瓜子或小菜供客人開胃、消遣。在法國餐廳，客人一入座，服務生卽端來用透明玻璃杯盛著的青菜沙拉，切成長條形的紅蘿蔔、黃瓜、及美國大芹菜等，不但脆而多汁，而且顏色鮮麗煞是好看。

　　沙拉以生食爲主，故講究新鮮、淸潔、冰冷，炎炎夏日尤其受人歡迎。在歐美有些人爲了減肥，午餐只點一客沙拉用以充饑。沙拉的生意太好了，因此餐廳也因應客人的喜好，備有種類繁多的沙拉菜單。材料不限於蔬菜、水果，舉凡雞胸肉、海鮮、通心粉、蛋及乾酪等都可以做沙拉。

常見的沙拉簡介：

* *Caesar's Salad* 凱撒沙拉

　　生菜中加入 cheese（乾酪）、crouton（油煎方型小麵包片）再拌以牛奶、雞蛋所製成。

* *Chef's Salad* 主廚沙拉

　　什錦生菜沙拉，配以主廚所選擇的乾酪或肉類切條做爲裝飾。

* *Coleslaw* 涼拌生菜絲

沙拉簡介

　　將捲心菜切成細絲，拌以葡萄乾或核桃仁，再用白沙拉醬調拌。

* *Chicken & Asparagus Salad* 雞肉蘆筍沙拉

　　雞胸肉切丁、蘆筍切丁，拌以開水燙過的洋菇、蘆筍尖，再用蛋黃醬（mayonnaise）調拌而成。

* *Shrimp Salad* 鮮蝦沙拉

　　水煮鮮蝦，拌以黃瓜切片、蛋、馬鈴薯、萵苣等，再用法式佐料（French Dressing）調拌。

* *Mixed Vegetable Salad* 綜合蔬菜沙拉

　　胡蘿蔔切丁，蕪菁切丁，水煮青豆，拌以馬鈴薯丁、半熟的甜菜和切片的煮蛋，用黑胡椒及蛋黃醬調拌。

* *Waldorf Salad* 華多夫沙拉

　　生蘋果切丁，拌以芹菜丁、胡桃（walnut），再用檸檬汁、鹽及蛋黃醬調味。

* *Fruit Salad* 水果沙拉

　　以水果代替蔬菜的沙拉，所用材料多為罐頭水果。

解釋菜單上的食物

Explaining the Menu

Dialogue : *W* = **Waiter** 服務生　　　*G* = **Guest** 客人

W : Good evening, sir. Here is the dinner menu.
先生，晚安。這是晚餐的菜單。

G : Thank you. What is the " *Chinese Chicken Kebab* " like ?
謝謝，"中國式烤雞肉串"是什麼樣的菜？

W : It is diced chicken with leek and small green peppers on
a skewer, *covered with a special sauce* and barbecued.
那是用串肉籤把韭菜、小綠辣椒和雞丁串在一起，塗上特製
的調味料烤出來的。

G : That sounds good. *How many are there per serving* ?
聽起來挺不錯。每一客有幾串？

W : There are three per serving. Will that be enough ?
一客三串。一客夠嗎？

G : I'll try them first and then order more if I need them.
What salads do you have ?
我先試試看，需要的話再點。你們有什麼樣的沙拉？

W：Mixed Salad, Seafood Salad and *Gourmandize Salad*.
綜合沙拉，海鮮沙拉和美食沙拉。

G：What is the Gourmandize Salad?
什麼是美食沙拉？

W：It is a mixed salad with smoked duck and orange slices.
It will be perfect with the Chicken Kebab.
是一種燻鴨和柳橙切片混合的沙拉。和串雞肉一起吃會很棒。

G：Fine. I'll try that then and I'll have a beer, too.
好，就試試看那種。我還要一瓶啤酒。

W：Would you like your salad *now or later*?
您的沙拉是現在要用還是等會兒再用？

G：I'll have it later. 等會兒再用。

W：Certainly, sir. A Gourmandize Salad, Chicken Kebab and
a bottle of beer. *Will there be anything else*?
好的，先生。一份美食沙拉，烤雞肉串和一瓶啤酒。還要別的
嗎？

G：No, that's all. 不，這樣就好。

W：Thank you, sir. Just a moment, please.
謝謝您，先生。請稍等一會兒。

活用例句精華

G・What kind of dish is it?

① It is a very light（filling）
dish.

② It is a bacon, tomato and let-
tuce sandwich.

③ *It is beef stewed in red wine.*

④ It is ～ sautéed with …….

⑤ It is ～ mixed with …….

⑥ *It has a very rich taste.*

⑦ It has a very delicate（*subtle*）
taste.

⑧ I'm afraid the gratin will take
about 15 *minutes to prepare*,
sir. Would you mind waiting?

⑨ sweet, sour, salty, hot／
spicy.

G・ 那是一道什麼樣的菜？

① 那是一道份量很少（多）
的菜。

② 那是一個有醃肉、蕃茄
和萵苣的三明治。

③ 那是用紅葡萄酒燉的牛
肉。

④ 那是用……炸的～。

⑤ 那是用……混合的～。

⑥ 這道菜口味很重。

⑦ 這道菜很美味（精緻）。

⑧ 先生，那道菜恐怕要花
十五分鐘來準備。您介
不介意等一下？

⑨ 甜的，酸的，鹹的，辣
的。

kebab〔kə'bæb〕n. 以小木棒交叉串起的烤肉

dice〔daɪs〕v. 將⋯切丁　　leek〔lik〕n. 韭荽

pepper〔'pɛpɚ〕n. 胡椒

skewer〔'skjuɚ〕n. 串肉籤

sauce〔sɔs〕n.(一種)調味汁

barbecue〔'bɑrbɪ,kju〕v. 烤(肉等)

serving〔'sɝvɪŋ〕n. 一客

gourmandize〔'gʊrmən,daɪz〕v. 縱情於美食

smoked〔smokt〕adj. 燻製的

duck〔dʌk〕n. 鴨

bacon〔'bekən〕n. 醃薰的豬肉

lettuce〔'lɛtɪs〕n. 萵苣　　stew〔stju〕v. 燉肉

sauté〔so'te〕v. 煎;炸;炒

delicate〔'dɛləkət〕adj. 精美的

subtle〔'sʌtl̩〕adj. 精緻的

gratin〔'grætn̩〕n. 該種菜餚

salty〔'sɔltɪ〕adj. 鹹的

spicy〔'spaɪsɪ〕adj. 辣的

向顧客推薦食物
Recommending Dishes
to the Guest

Dialogue: *W* = **Waiter** 服務生   *G* = **Guest** 客人

W : Good evening, sir. Here is the menu.
　　先生，晚安。這是菜單。

G : Thank you. ***By the way***, I've just been to the Dentist's
　　and so I'd like something which doesn't require chewing.
　　謝謝，對了，我剛去看過牙醫，所以我要不須咀嚼的食物。

W : ***Is there anything you cannot eat*** ?
　　有什麼東西您不能吃的嗎？

G : No. 沒有。

W : I see. How about the Steamed Pomfret in Oil, the Chef's
　　Recommendation for today.
　　我知道了。來一道油浸鯧魚如何？這是今天主廚的推薦菜。

G : I had fish for lunch so ***I'd like to try something else***.
　　我中午吃過魚了，所以我想吃點別的。

W : How about the Ham Slices Glazed with Honey Sauce ?
蜜汁火腿如何？

G : Fine, I'll have that. What is the soup of the day ?
好的，我就點這個。今天有什麼湯？

W : It's Bamboo Shoot Soup, sir.
雪筍湯，先生。

G : Great. *It's my favorite*. I'll have that.
很好，那是我最喜歡的。我就點這個。

W : Would you like rolls with your soup ?
您要來點小圓麵包配湯嗎？

G : No, that's all. I'm trying to *lose weight*.
不，那樣就好。我正想減肥。

W : Thank you, sir. Just a moment, please.
先生，謝謝。請稍等一會兒。

活用例句精華

① Are you *on a special diet*, ma'am?

① 夫人，您有什麼特別限定的飲食嗎？

② This dish contains pork.

② 這道菜有豬肉。

③ Are you *in a hurry*?

③ 您趕時間嗎？

④ If you are in a hurry, I would recommend the spaghetti or the pilaff.

④ 如果您趕時間的話。我推薦義大利麵條或肉飯。

⑤ I'm afraid vegetables are not included with the main dish. Could you order them separately, please?

⑤ 蔬菜恐怕不包括在主菜裡。請另外點,好嗎?

⑥ When shall I bring your salad, sir?

⑥ 先生,該什麼時候上沙拉呢?

⑦ *Shall I cancel the order*, sir?

⑦ 先生,我可以刪掉這道菜嗎?

⑧ I recommend the ~, sir.

⑧ 先生,我推薦~。

⑨ *The set course will not take as much time.*

⑨ 和菜不會花那麼多時間。

⑩ I would recommend that you order a set course for 10 persons.

⑩ 我推薦您點十人份的和菜。

---

by the way "順便提起"

dentist 〔'dɛntɪst〕 *n.* 牙科醫生

pomfret 〔'pɑmfrɪt〕 *n.* 鯧魚　　chef 〔ʃɛf〕 *n.* 主廚

recommendation 〔ˌrɛkəmɛn'deʃən〕 *n.* 推薦

glaze 〔glez〕 *v.* 使…光滑　　bamboo 〔bæm'bu〕 *n.* 竹

favorite 〔'fevərɪt〕 *n.* 最喜愛之人或物

roll 〔rol〕 *n.* 一種小的圓形軟麵包

lose weight "減肥"

diet 〔'daɪət〕 *n.* (為養病或調節體重而限制的) 規定的飲食

contain 〔kən'ten〕 *v.* 包含　　pork 〔pork〕 *n.* 豬肉

spaghetti 〔spə'gɛtɪ〕 *n.* 義大利式麵條

pilaff 〔pə'lɑf〕 *n.* 肉飯 (米中加肉、魚及香料等)

cancel 〔'kænsl̩〕 *v.* 刪除

用餐時的服務

上菜的順序如下：

　　1.麵包（ bread ）　　2.開胃菜（ appetizers ）

　　3.湯（ soup ）　　4.主菜：魚肉類（fish and meat ）

　　5.點心（ dessert ）6.咖啡或紅茶（coffee or tea ）

用餐前、進餐時、用餐後，均可飲用酒類，若客人自行帶酒，通常會酌收開瓶費。

　　有經驗的服務生除了上菜，收拾餐盤外，還會主動詢問客人對餐點的味道及烹調方式的感覺，例如 " *How is your meal?* " 或 " *Are you enjoying your meal, sir?* " 並利用機會推薦開胃酒、甜點、水果等，以增加客人的消費額。

　　有時，難免會有客人要求替他做一些額外的服務，若無法辦到時，可以 "I'm afraid *I'm not allowed to leave my post.*" 加以婉拒。

　　餐畢結帳時，帳單要用小盤子盛著再送上去。如果客人不付現，要簽單時，為避免認不出姓名，可以請他用印刷體寫 " *Please write your name in block letters.*" 或 "*Please print your name, sir.* "。

　　用餐時的服務，最重要的是不忘隨時面帶笑容。冷硬刻板的臉孔會減損食物的美味，使食物不易消化，微笑才是萬國通用的語言。

用餐時的服務

Service during the Meal

Dialogue: *W* = **Waiter** 服務生　　*G* = **Guest** 客人

W: Your steak, salad and beer, sir. Please enjoy your lunch.
先生，您的牛排、沙拉和啤酒。請慢用。

....

W: Excuse me, *may I take your plate*, sir?
對不起，先生，我可以把盤子收起來嗎？

G: Sure, *go ahead*. 好的，請便。

W: May I show you the dessert menu?
您要看甜點的菜單嗎？

G: Yes, please. 好的。

W: Here you are, sir. 請看。

G: Let's see. I'll have some ice cream, please.
嗯，我要一些冰淇淋。

W : *Which flavor would you prefer*, walnut or vanilla?
　　您喜歡哪一種口味的，核桃還是香草？

G : I'll take the walnut, please.
　　請給我核桃的。

W : Certainly, sir. Just a moment, please.
　　好的，先生。請稍等一會兒。

．．．

W : Your ice cream and coffee, sir. Will that be all?
　　先生，您的冰淇淋和咖啡。就這些嗎？

G : Yes. 是的。

W : Thank you, sir. *Have a nice afternoon*.
　　謝謝您，先生。祝您有個愉快的下午。

G : Thanks, I will. 謝謝。

活用例句精華

① Have you finished your meal, sir?

① 先生，您用完餐了嗎？

② This dish is very hot. *Please be careful*.

② 這道菜很燙，請小心。

③ May I move your plate to the side?

③ 我可以把盤子移到一邊去嗎？

④ *May I serve it to you now*?

④ 我可以現在上菜嗎？

⑤ Would you like some coffee ?

⑤ 您要來點兒咖啡嗎？

⑥ How is your meal ?

⑥ 這些菜的味道如何？

⑦ Are you enjoying your meal, sir ?

⑦ 先生，您喜歡這一餐嗎？

⑧ *May I clean (clear) the table,* sir ?

⑧ 先生，我可以收拾桌子了嗎？

⑨ May I wipe the counter, sir ?

⑨ 先生，我可以擦櫃枱了嗎？

⑩ *This is our last service for coffee.* Would you like some more ?

⑩ 咖啡是我們最後的服務了，您還要什麼嗎？

⑪ We are taking the last orders for food (drinks). Will there be anything else ?

⑪ 這道食物（飲料）是最後一道菜了，還要別的嗎？

⑫ *On whose check* (bill) would you like me to put the drinks order ?

⑫ 您點的飲料要由誰付帳呢？

⑬ *This food is best eaten while hot.* Please enjoy your meal.

⑬ 這食物最好趁熱吃。請好好享用。

---

plate〔plet〕*n.* 盤；碟   *go ahead* "進行；先請"
flavor〔'fleva〕*n.* 味道   walnut〔'wɔlnət〕*n.* 核桃
vanilla〔və'nɪlə〕*n.* 香草   meal〔mil〕*n.* 一餐
wipe〔waɪp〕*v.* 擦拭   counter〔'kaʊntə〕*n.* 櫃枱

出售香煙

Cigarette Sales

Dialogue： *G* = **Guest** 客人　　*W* = **Waiter** 服務生

G : Could you bring me some cigarettes, please ?

請拿煙給我，好嗎？

W : *Which brand would you prefer* ?

您喜歡什麼牌子的？

G : I'd like Salem Menthol, please.

請給我雪樂的薄荷煙。

W : I'm afraid we only stock Lark Regular or Mild, sir.

先生，我恐怕我們只存有一般長短的或淡味的雲雀煙。

G : Well, *make it Regular then*.

嗯，那麼拿一般長短的來！

W : Certainly, sir, but I'm afraid *they must be paid for separately*.

好的，先生。但是香煙恐怕得分開付帳。

G : Can't you just put it on my bill ?

　　不能算進我的帳單裡嗎？

W : I'm afraid we keep a separate record for cigarette sales.

　　我們對香煙的售賣恐怕得分開記錄。

G : Well, how much are they ?

　　好吧，要多少錢？

W : NT$ 190, sir. 台幣一百九十元，先生。

G : Here you are then. 那麼拿去吧。

W : Excuse me, sir. Your cigarettes and change.

　　對不起，這是您的香煙和零錢。

G : Thanks a lot. 謝謝。

W : You're welcome, sir. 不客氣。

cigarette〔'sɪgə,rɛt〕 *n.* 香煙
menthol〔'mɛnθol〕 *n.* 薄荷腦
stock〔stɑk〕 *v.* 貯存
regular〔'rɛgjələ〕 *adj.* 一般長短的
pay〔pe〕 *v.* 付費　　record〔'rɛkəd〕 *n.* 記錄
change〔tʃendʒ〕 *n.* 零錢

客人離開餐廳時

① Have a nice day (*afternoon,* *evening*), sir.

① 先生,祝您有個愉快的日子(下午,夜晚)!

② Thank you for dining with us. Please come again.

② 謝謝您在本餐廳用餐,請再度光臨。

③ I hope you enjoyed your meal. Please come again.

③ 希望您用餐還愉快,請再度光臨。

④ *Hope to see you again soon.*

④ 希望很快能再見到您。

⑤ It's a pleasure to serve you and your family again.

⑤ 很樂意再為您和您家人服務。

⑥ We *look forward to* seeing you again, sir.

We *look forward to* serving you again, sir.

⑥ 我們期待再見到您。

我們期待能再為您服務。

⑦ We hope to welcome you again.

⑦ 我們希望能再次歡迎您。

⑧ Could you pay at the Cashier's Desk *at the entrance*, please?

⑧ 請到門口的出納櫃枱付款,好嗎?

⑨ It's very kind of you, sir, but I'm afraid we cannot accept tips. A 10% service charge has already been added to your bill.

⑨ 您真是太好了,但是我們恐怕不能收小費。您的帳單上已經添加了百分之十的服務費。

⑩ Well, if you insist, sir. Thank you very much indeed.

⑩ 好吧，先生，如果您堅持的話。實在非常感謝。

⑪ You may pay *at your table*, sir.

⑪ 先生，您可以在座位上付費。

dine〔daɪn〕*v.* 用餐
pleasure〔'plɛʒɚ〕*n.* 愉快
look forward to "期待"
cashier〔kæ'ʃɪr〕*n.* 出納員
accept〔ək'sɛpt〕*v.* 接受　　tip〔tɪp〕*n.* 小費
insist〔ɪn'sɪst〕*v.* 堅持；強調
indeed〔ɪn'did〕*adv.* 的確；實在

佐餐葡萄酒須知

　　葡萄酒因有獨特的香味，所以有些料理搭配起來會不對味。推薦葡萄酒給客人之前，或選擇酒類佐餐時，必須先具備以下的知識。

1. 提供給客人的次序最好由淡酒而烈酒，先辛辣而甘甜，先白葡萄酒而後紅葡萄酒。

2. 進餐中飲用的葡萄酒種類最好不要太多，1～3種好酒最為恰當。

3. 香檳可當作餐前酒，也可以搭配食物佐餐，但還是以當餐後酒為佳。

4. 甜味的酒類通常搭配點心類食物。

5. **沙拉**類食物不適合與酒搭配飲用。

6. 有醋、酸黃瓜、咖哩、芥茉等調味的食物，不適合與酒搭配飲用。

7. 湯（soup）只能選擇不甜的雪莉酒（Dry Sherry）或不甜的白葡萄酒（Madeira）一起飲用。

8. 蔬菜可與任何酒類搭配，但是吃**胡蘿蔔**以後，**會使白葡萄酒變得帶有酸味**，吃**菠菜**以後，**會使中等甜度**（semi-dry）**的酒類嚐起來像甜酒**。

9. 吃乾酪（cheese）時，搭配紅酒比搭配白酒適宜。

推薦開胃酒

Recommending an Aperitif

Dialogue : *S* = **Sommelier** 酒保　　*G₁* = **a Male Guest** 男客
　　　　　　G₂ = **a Female Guest** 女客

S : Good evening. It's very nice to see you again.
　　　晚安。歡迎再度光臨。

G₁ : Thank you. It's good to be back.
　　　謝謝。再來這裏感覺眞好。

S : *Would you care for an apéritif before your meal* ?
　　　進餐前要不要來杯開胃酒？

G₁ : Yes, I think we will. In fact, today we have something to
　　　celebrate. I've just been promoted to Area Sales Manager.
　　　是的，我們要。事實上，今天我們有事要慶祝。我剛升爲地區
　　　的行銷經理。

S : That's wonderful！Congratulations, sir！
　　　太棒了！先生，恭禧您。

G₁ : *I think it calls for something special*. What would you
　　　recommend？
　　　我想需要特別一點的東西。可否推薦一下？

S : How about a Champagne Cocktail for madam and a Kirsch for you, sir?

　　先生，叫香檳雞尾酒給夫人，您點櫻桃酒如何？

G₁ : What would you like, dear?

　　親愛的，你想要什麼？

G₂ : The Champagne Cocktail sounds delicious. I'll try that.

　　香檳雞尾酒聽起來很棒，我想嚐嚐看。

G₁ : *I think I'll have a Dry Sherry instead of the Kirsch.*

　　我要一杯沒有甜味的雪莉酒，不要櫻桃酒。

S : Certainly, sir. A Champagne Cocktail for madam and a Dry Sherry for you. Just a moment, please.

　　好的，先生。夫人要香檳雞尾酒，您要沒有甜味的雪莉酒，請稍待一會兒。

活用例句精華

① Since it is your wedding anniversary, how about champagne, sir?

①先生，既然今天是您的結婚周年紀念，來瓶香檳酒如何？

② A Dry Sherry and Kirsch *are* both very *popular with* our guests.

②沒有甜味的雪利酒和櫻桃酒兩種都很受我們客人喜愛。

③ *Would you like to try the sherry recommended by our Chef*?

③您想不想嚐嚐我們主廚所推薦的雪莉酒？

apéritif 〔ɑperi'tif〕*n.* 〔法〕開胃酒；飯前酒（供促進食慾者）

celebrate 〔'sɛlə,bret〕*v.* 慶祝

congratulations 〔kən,grætʃə'leʃənz〕*n.* 祝賀；恭禧

call for "需要；要求"

champagne 〔ʃæm'pen〕*n.* 香檳酒

Kirsch 〔kɪrʃ〕*n.* 櫻桃酒

dry 〔draɪ〕*adj.* （葡萄酒等）無甜味的（通常指比較濃的）

sherry 〔'ʃɛrɪ〕*n.* 雪莉酒（西班牙南部原產的白葡萄酒）

wedding 〔'wɛdɪŋ〕*n.* 結婚；婚禮

anniversary 〔,ænə'vɝsərɪ〕*n.* 周年紀念

chef 〔ʃɛf〕*n.* 主廚

兜售酒類飲料

Wine Sales

Dialogue： *S* = **Sommelier** 酒保　　*G* = **Guest** 客人

S： Good evening, sir. ***Would you like to order some wine with
your meal***?

　　先生，晚安。您想不想叫點酒配食物？

G： Um, yes. 嗯，好吧。

S： The wine list, sir. 先生，這是酒牌。

G： Thank you. You certainly have a very extensive cellar. What
would you recommend？

　　謝謝。你們的藏酒的確非常豐富。可否推薦一下？

S： I think that a Chablis or a Muscatel would *go very well
with* your oysters.

　　我想白葡萄酒或是麝香葡萄酒和您點的牡蠣會很相配。

G： ***We'd like one which is very dry.***

　　我們想要一點也沒有甜味的。

S： Then I would recommend the Muscatel.

　　那麼我推薦麝香葡萄酒。

G：Fine, we'll take a half bottle of that then.
好，那麼我們就叫半瓶。

S：And with your steak？ 點什麼來配牛排呢？

G：Let's see, *do you have a very full-bodied wine which is not too fruity*？
我想想看，你們有沒有很濃郁但不會有太多水果味的酒？

S：Our own house wine which we import specially, the Château de Lescours, would be very suitable. *It is a Burgundy with a rich but delicate body* which is not too dry.
我們自己特別進口的招牌酒，沙脫得拉斯寇就很適合。那是一種濃郁而美味的布根地酒，也不致太沒有甜味。

G：That sounds just right. We'll have a full bottle of that.
那聽起來正適合。我們就叫一整瓶。

S：Certainly, sir. Just a moment, please.
好的，先生。請稍待一會兒。

活用例句精華

① I think this would fall within your price range.

① 我想這會在您預定的價錢範圍內。

②*Which vintage would you prefer*？

② 您喜歡哪一種葡萄酒？

③ The dish you ordered is very delicate (*subtle / rich*) in taste.

③ 您點的菜味道非常精美（淡／油膩）。

④ This wine goes very well with white fish.

④ 這種酒非常適合白魚。

extensive〔ɪkˈstɛnsɪv〕*adj.* 大量的；廣泛的

cellar〔ˈsɛlɚ〕*n.* 藏酒；酒窖

chablis〔ˈʃæblɪ；ʃɑˈbli〕*n.* 法國 Chablis 地方所產的一種白
葡萄酒

Muscatel〔͵mʌskəˈtɛl；ˈmʌskə͵tɛl〕*n.* 麝香葡萄酒（產於
法、義等國之）一種芳香有甜味的白葡萄酒

go very well with~ "和~很相配"

full-bodied〔ˈfʊlˈbɑdɪd〕*adj.*（酒等）濃郁而強烈的

vintage〔ˈvɪntɪdʒ〕*n.* 葡萄酒（尤指某一特別地區一年所產者）

subtle〔ˈsʌtl̩〕*adj.* 淡薄的

酒類飲料的服務

Wine Service

Dialogue： *S* = **Sommelier** 酒保　　　*G* = **Guest** 客人

S：Your Muscatel, sir. *May I serve it now*？
　　先生，您的麝香葡萄酒，現在可以倒酒了嗎？

G：Yes, please. 好的，請倒。

S：How is it, sir？ 先生，味道如何？

G：It has a very interesting bouquet.
　　有種很有趣的香味。

S：Will this be all right？ 這酒還可以嗎？

G：Yes, it's just fine. 是的，剛剛好。

S：Thank you, sir. 謝謝您，先生。

　　　　···

S：Your red Burgundy, sir. Would you like to taste it？
　　先生，您的布根地紅酒，要不要嚐嚐看？

G：Yes. 好的。

S：（*Pours wine*）How is it, sir？ （倒酒）先生，味道如何？

G : Very good.　非常好。

S : *May I decant it now to allow it to breathe*?
　　我現在可不可以慢慢倒，好讓香味散出來？

G : Yes, do that.　好的，就這麼做。

S : Thank you, sir. Please enjoy your meal.
　　先生，謝謝。請慢用。

活用例句精華

① *I'll put the cork here.*

② How is the temperature (*bouquet / taste / color*) of the wine?

③ May I serve the Côtes du Rhône now, sir?

④ I think that the Bordeaux should *be decanted* now and *allowed to breathe for a little while.*

G・There's a lot of *sediment* in the bottle.

・*This wine tastes of the cork.*

・This wine tastes very vinegary (*tart*).

・*This wine is not chilled enough.*

① 我把軟木塞放在這兒。

② 酒的溫度（香味／味道／顏色）如何？

③ 先生，現在可以上玫瑰酒了嗎？

④ 我認為現在波爾多酒應該輕輕倒，好讓氣味發散一下。

G・瓶子裏有許多沈澱物。

・這酒喝起來有軟木塞的味道。

・這酒喝起來很酸(辛辣)。

・這酒不夠冰。

bouquet〔bu´ke〕*n.* 香味

decant〔dɪ´kænt〕*v.* 把（上面的清液）慢慢倒出（使不震動原容器中的沈澱物）

breathe〔brið〕*v.* 飄香；發出香味　　cork〔kɔrk〕*n.* 軟木塞

Bordeaux〔bɔr´do〕*n.* 波爾多酒

sediment〔´sɛdəmənt〕*n.* 沈澱物

vinegary〔´vɪnɪgərɪ〕*adj.* 酸溜溜的

tart〔tɑrt〕*adj.* 辛辣的；酸的

推薦利口酒

Recommending a Liqueur

Dialogue： *S* = **Sommelier** 酒保　　*G* = **Guest** 客人

S：Did you enjoy your meal, sir？　先生，您吃得愉快嗎？

G：Yes, it was great. The wine was excellent. It went very
well with the steak. 是的，非常好。酒很棒，和牛排很相配。

S：Thank you, sir. The harp recital will be beginning very
soon. ***Would you like a liqueur to complete your meal***？
謝謝。豎琴獨奏的表演很快就開始。您要不要叫點利口酒來結束
這頓飯？

G：Yes, a Grand Marnier for my wife and I'll have a brandy,
please. 好的，請給我太太一杯格蘭瑪娜，我要一杯白蘭地。

S：Certainly, sir. ***Which brand would you prefer***？
好的，先生。請問您要什麼牌子的？

G：I'll have a Rémy Martin V.S.O.P., please.
我要一杯人頭馬白蘭地。

S：Certainly, sir. Just a moment, please.
好的，先生。請稍等一會。

食物外帶須知

速食店、咖啡店或甚至部份餐廳都有外帶（ take out）的服務。此時只要在點叫的東西後面加上 to go 或 to take out 卽可。

" I want two hamburgers, one plain, the other with all trimmings *to go.* "

我要兩個漢堡帶走，一個什麼都不加，另一個全部的佐料都要。

" I want two coffees, one black, the other with cream *to take out.* "

我要兩杯咖啡帶走，一杯不加糖不加奶精，另一杯只加奶精。

服務生的回答通常是 " All right. *I'll put them in paper cups*（ brown paper bags ）. "「好的，我把它們放進紙杯子裏（牛皮紙帶裏）」。

如果需要多拿幾根吸管或幾張餐巾，則說 "*May I have several more straws（ napkins ）?* "有些店裏則由客人自行取拿。

標準買單付款方式

Standard Bill Payment

Dialogue： *C* = **Cashier** 出納員　　*G* = **Guest** 客人

C : Good evening, sir. May I help you？
　　先生，晚安。要結帳嗎？

G : Yes, how much will this be？
　　這帳單多少錢？

C : Just a moment, please. I'll calculate that for you.
　　Thank you for waiting, sir. ***Your bill comes to*** NT$13,450.
　　請稍等一會，我計算一下。
　　勞您久等了，先生。您的帳單總共是新台幣一萬三千四百五十元。

G : Fine. Will this be enough？　好，這樣夠嗎？

C : No, that's too much, sir. NT$15,000 will be enough. ***Here***
　　is your change of NT$1,550.
　　不，太多了。一萬五千元台幣就夠了。這是找您的零錢一千五百
　　五十元。

G : Thanks.　謝謝。

C : Thank you, sir. Have a nice evening.　謝謝，祝您晚上過得愉快。

活用例句精華

① I'm afraid that won't be enough.

① 那樣恐怕不夠。

〔 *Points to remember for the Restaurant Cashier* 〕

〔 餐廳出納員應注意事項 〕

1. Remember to tell the guest *the amount of the bill*, " *Thirteen thousand, four hundred and fifty N.T. Dollars.*"

1. 記得告訴客人帳單的總額，"新台幣一萬三千四百五十元"。

2. Tell the guest *how much you received*, " *Fifteen thousand N.T. Dollars.*"

2. 告訴客人你收到多少錢，"新台幣一萬五千元"。

3. Tell the guest *the amount of the change*, " *One thousand five hundred and fifty N.T. Dollars.*"

3. 告訴客人零錢的總額，"一千五百五十元"。

4. If possible, *count the change* in front of the guest.

   For example :

   " *Here is your change of NT $ 1,550, sir.*

   Thirteen thousand five hundred,

   Fourteen thousand,

   Fifteen thousand N.T. Dollars."

4. 如果可能，當著客人面前數零錢給客人。

   例如：

   "先生，這是找您的零錢台幣一千五百五十元。

   一萬三千五百元，

   一萬四千元，

   一萬五千元台幣。"

解釋稅率和服務費

Explaining the Tax
and Service Charges

Dialogue： *C* = **Cashier** 出納員　　*G* = **Guest** 客人

C ： Good afternoon, sir. May I help you ?

午安，先生，要結帳嗎？

G ： Yes, *I'd like to settle my bill*, please. How much is it ?

是的，我要買單。一共多少？

C ： Thank you, sir. Your bill comes to NT$4,800.

謝謝，一共是台幣四千八百元。

G ： *Are you sure that's right* ? *Shouldn't it be* NT$4,000 ?

你確定沒錯嗎？不是應該台幣四千元嗎？

C ： I'm afraid there is a 10% tax and a 10% service charge.

恐怕還得加上百分之十的稅和百分之十的服務費。

G ： Well, that's a nuisance. I only have about NT$4,500. *Do
you take traveller's cheques* ?

哦，真糟糕！我只有大約四千五百元台幣而已，你們收不收旅行
支票呢？

C : I'm afraid we do not accept them here. You may change them at the Exchange Counter in the Lobby.

我們這裏恐怕不收旅行支票。您可以在大廳的滙兌櫃枱兌換。

G : Well, what about ～ credit cards?

嗯，那麼～公司的信用卡呢？

C : I'm afraid *we do not accept ～ cards* but we do accept these. (*Points to credit card display*)

我們恐怕不接受～公司的信用卡，但我們接受這些。（指向信用卡的陳列板）

G : How am I going to pay the bill then?

那麼我怎麼付帳單呢？

C : *Are you a staying guest*, sir?

先生，您住在本飯店嗎？

G : Yes, I am. 是的。

C : Could you sign the bill and add your room number, please? *The amount will be added to your final room bill.*

請在帳單上簽名並寫上房間號碼。總額會加在您最後的客房帳單上。

G : I see. Here you are.

我知道了，這給你。

C : Thank you, sir. May I see your room key, please?

先生，謝謝。讓我看看您房間的鑰匙好嗎？

G : Here it is. 這就是。

C : Thank you, sir. We hope you enjoyed your meal.

謝謝，希望您用餐還愉快。

活用例句精華

① A 10％ tax and a 10％ service charge *have been added to* your bill.

① 百分之十的稅和百分之十的服務費已經加在您的帳單上了。

② Your bill includes a 10％ tax and a 10％ service charge.

② 您的帳單包括了百分之十的稅和百分之十的服務費。

③ I'm afraid we do not accept personal checks here.

③ 我們這裏恐怕不收私人支票。

④ I'm afraid we cannot *honor traveller's checks* here.

④ 我們這裏恐怕不承兌旅行支票。

⑤ I'm afraid *we cannot accept foreign currency as payment* here.

⑤ 我們這裏恐怕不接受用外幣付帳。

⑥ We accept the credit cards displayed here.

⑥ 我們接受列在這裏的信用卡。

⑦ *May I take a print of your card*?

⑦ 我可以劃印您的信用卡嗎?

⑧ I'm afraid there is a cover charge of NT$100 after 8 p.m. when there is a band.

⑧ 裏頭恐怕包括了晚上八點以後樂隊演奏的服務費一百元台幣。

⑨ *There is no cover charge for* seats at the bar.

⑨ 酒吧裏的座位不收服務費。

⑩ Could you show me your room key, please?

⑩ 請給我看您的房間鑰匙, 好嗎?

⑪ Do you have your room key with you, sir?

⑪ 先生,您的房間鑰匙帶在身上嗎?

G‧Yes, but *why do you want to see it?*

G‧是的,但是你爲什麼要看呢?

⑫ *We might charge the bill to the wrong room by mistake.*

⑫ 我們可能把帳單算錯房間了。

---

settle〔'sɛtl〕*vt.* 支付;算清

nuisance〔'n(j)usns〕*n.* 麻煩的事

cheque〔tʃɛk〕*n.*〔英〕支票　　lobby〔'labɪ〕*n.* 前廳

honor〔'anɚ〕*v.* 接受　　currency〔'kɝənsɪ〕*n.* 貨幣

cover charge (餐館、夜總會等所定,除飲食品之外加收的)
服務費;娛樂費

當餐券不夠付餐費時

When the Food Voucher
Doesn't Cover the Cost of the Meal

Dialogue: *G* = **Guest** 客人　　*C* = **Cashier** 出納員

G : *Can I use this voucher to pay for my meal*？
　　我可以用這張餐券付餐費嗎？

C : Certainly, sir, but I'm afraid it will not cover the cost of
the meal. *Would you mind paying the extra in cash*, please？
　　當然可以，先生，只是恐怕還不夠，您介意剩下的用現金支付嗎？

G : Not at all. How much is the voucher worth？
　　一點也不。這餐券值多少錢？

C : It is worth NT$2,000 and your bill comes to NT$2,800.
The difference is NT$800, please.
　　值台幣二千元，而您的帳單一共是二千八百元。請給差額八百元。

G : Here you are.　錢在這裏。

C : Thank you, sir. Could you sign the voucher here, please？
　　謝謝您。請在這張餐券上簽名，好嗎？

G : Why do I have to sign？
　　爲什麼要簽名？

C : I'm afraid *the travel agent requires your signature.*
    旅行社恐怕需要您的簽名。

G : I see. Here you are.
    我知道了。簽好了。

C : Thank you, sir. Hope to see you again soon.
    謝謝,先生。希望很快再見到您。

活用例句精華

① *To receive payment from the travel agent*, we require your signature.

① 爲了能收到旅行社的付款,我們需要您的簽名。

② The value of your food voucher is NT$2,000.

② 您這張餐券的價值是台幣二千元。

③ Would you mind paying the extra *on a separate check*?

③ 您介意用另一張支票付多餘的金額嗎?

---

voucher 〔'vaʊtʃɚ〕 n. (金錢的)收據
extra 〔'ɛkstrə〕 adj. 額外的
agent 〔'edʒənt〕 n. 代辦人
signature 〔'sɪgnətʃɚ〕 n. 簽字

找錯錢給客人時

Giving a Guest
the Wrong Change

Dialogue : *G* = **Guest** 客人　　*C* = **Cashier** 出納員

G : Excuse me, but I think *you've overcharged me.*
　　對不起，我認爲你多算了我的費用。

C : I'm very sorry, sir. May I see your bill, please ?
　　對不起。請給我看看您的帳單好嗎？

G : Here you are.　在這裏。

C : How much change did I give you, sir ?
　　我找多少錢給您，先生？

G : *You gave me* NT$3,000 *instead of* NT$4,000.
　　你找我三千元而不是四千元。

C : *I'm very sorry for the mistake. Here is the right change.*
　　很抱歉我弄錯了。這裏是正確的零錢。

G : Thanks a lot.
　　謝謝。

C : Thank you very much. Please come again.
　　非常謝謝，請再來。

活用例句精華

① I'll check our accounts. Just a moment, please.

① 我查一查帳單。請稍等一下。

② Excuse me, sir, *but you gave me a* NT$500 *note and not a* NT$1,000 *note*.

② 對不起,先生,你給我的是五百元鈔票而不是一千元鈔票。

③ Could you check again, please, sir?

③ 先生,請再檢查一下好嗎?

---

overcharge 〔'ovɚ'tʃardʒ〕 *vt.* 計價過高

指示方向

Giving Directions

Dialogue ❶：*G* = **Guest** 客人　　*W* = **Waiter** 服務生

G : Excuse me, where is the telephone?
　　對不起，請問哪裏有電話。

W : The *public phone*, ma'am? 公共電話嗎，太太？

G : Yes. 是的

W : It's over there *at the back of the elevator hall*.
　　就在電梯間的後方。

G : Thanks a lot. 多謝。

W : You're welcome, ma'am. 不客氣，太太。

Dialogue ❷：

G : Could you please tell me how to get to the Bar?
　　請告訴我如何去酒吧好嗎？

W : The Bar is on this floor. Please *go straight along the*
　　hallway, turn right at the end and the Bar is *on the left*.
　　酒吧就在這一樓。請沿著走廊直走，到盡頭右轉，酒吧就在左方。

G : Thank you. 謝謝你。

活用例句精華

① The cloakroom is over there.

① 洗手間就在那邊。

② The elevators are straight ahead *on the left*.

② 電梯在正前方的左邊。

③ The restroom is at the end of the hallway *to the right*.

③ 洗手間在走廊盡頭右轉的地方。

④ The stairway is *around the corner* over there.

④ 樓梯就在那邊的轉角處。

⑤ It is rather complicated. *I'll show you the way*.

⑤ 這相當複雜。我帶你去好了。

---

public〔'pʌblɪk〕*adj.* 公共的
over there "在那裡" elevator〔'ɛlə,vetɚ〕*n.*電梯
straight〔stret〕*adv.* 直地
hallway〔'hɔl,we〕*n.* 走廊
cloakroom〔'klok,rum〕*n.* 盥洗室；衣帽間
restroom〔'rɛst,rum〕*n.* 洗手間
stairway〔'stɛr,we〕*n.* 樓梯
complicated〔'kɑmplə,ketɪd〕*adj.* 複雜的

5

專門料理店的應對技巧
Conversation in a Speciality Restaurant

專門料理店的應對原則

　　不管是廣東菜、四川菜、北平菜或日本菜、鐵板燒（*Tepp-anyaki*），對歐美人士來說，都具有東方食物的新奇感。因此，服務生在服務時，**需特別偏重對各類菜點的介紹**，舉凡調味、製作方法、食物內容材料等，最好能流暢且詳細地向客人解說清楚。此外，西方人對我們使用的筷子（ *chopsticks* ）也相當好奇，多半都不會使用，所以最好利用機會介紹介紹。

　　東方菜肴通常都分為和菜（ *set courses* ）和菜單點菜（ *à la carte*）二種。由於合菜有固定的份量，要特別注意人數和菜量是否配合，如果不配合的話，要向客人解釋 " *I'm afraid this course is for four*（ *five, six ……* ）*persons.* 以免菜量太多吃不完。

　　這時客人也許會要求推薦合適的菜點，那麼就可以盡你所知，將餐廳裏膾炙人口的菜肴提供對方參考，必要時再附加一些解說。向客人推薦的菜式最好仍然以偏向一般歐美口味為主，以免客人吃不習慣，入不了口，自己吃力不討好了。畢竟人的胃口還是相當保守的。中國留學生出國時，還不是隨身帶個大同電鍋。

受理中餐的點菜

Taking the Order of Chinese Cuisine

Dialogue : *W* = **Waiter** 服務生　　*G* = **Guest** 客人

(*After showing two guests to their table*)
（帶領兩位客人入座之後）

W : Good afternoon. May I take your order?
午安，要點什麼菜？

G : *We'd like this course for two*, please.
這道菜請給我們來兩人份的。

W : I'm afraid this course is for four persons.
這道菜恐怕是四人份的。

G : Well, can't you make it for two only?
嗯，你們不能只做兩人份的嗎？

W : I'm afraid not, sir. This course is *for a minimum of* 4 to
5 persons and I think the portions will be too large for two.
先生，恐怕不行。這道菜至少是四到五個人吃的，我想這對兩個
人會太多了。

G : I see. Well, *what do you recommend then*?
我知道了，那麼點什麼好呢？

W： I would recommend a soup or an *appetizer* with two or three small dishes.

我建議您來碗湯或開胃菜和兩、三樣小菜。

G： Right, we'll have *the Sliced Chicken in Wine* and *Black Mushroom Soup* with this and this to follow.

好吧！我們要香糟雞片、香菇湯，還有這個和這個。

W： Certainly, sir. *Would you like large or small portions*?

好的，先生。您要大碗的還是小碗的。

G： I think the small portions will be enough. 我想小的就夠了。

W： Would you like rice with your meal?

您要白飯嗎？

G： No, thanks. 不要，謝謝。

W： (*Repeats order*) Thank you, sir. Just a moment, please.

（重覆所點的菜）謝謝您，先生。馬上就來。

活用例句精華

① Would you like a table in the main restaurant or *in a private room*?

①您喜歡主廳的座位，還是個別的餐室？

② I'm afraid *all the private rooms are reserved*. Would you mind a table in the main restaurant?

②恐怕所有個別的餐室都被訂光了，您不介意在主廳用餐吧？

③ One of the private rooms will be *available in about 10 minutes*. Would you mind waiting until then?

③有一間餐室在十分鐘後會空出來，您介不介意等到那時候？

④ I think this course will be suitable for four persons.

④ 我認爲這道菜適合四個人吃。

⑤ I think *the Chef should be able to make this.* I'll check with him. Just a moment, please.

⑤ 我想厨師應該會做這道菜，我問他看看，請等一下。

⑥ I'm afraid *we have no courses for one person.* Could you order from the *à la carte* menu, please?

⑥ 我們恐怕没有一人份的和菜，請照菜單點菜好嗎？

⑦ I would recommend the *Sweet and Sour Spareribs* if you like Spareribs dishes.

⑦ 我建議如果您喜歡排骨的話，不妨來個糖醋排骨。

⑧ I think that will be too much for two persons. It would be better to *reduce the number by two dishes.*

⑧ 我想那對兩個人來說太多了，減少兩道菜比較好。

⑨ Which dishes would you like to be served first？

⑨ 您要先上哪道菜？

---

minimum〔'mɪnəməm〕*n.* 最小量；最低額
portion〔'porʃən〕*n.*(食物的) 一客；一份
recommend〔,rɛkə'mɛnd〕*v.* 推薦；建議
appetizer〔'æpə,taɪzə〕*n.* 開胃的食物
sliced〔slaɪst〕*adj.*切成薄片的　　mushroom〔'mʌʃrum〕*n.*香菇
private〔'praɪvɪt〕*adj.* 自用的　　reserve〔rɪ'zɝv〕*v.* 預訂
available〔ə'veləb!〕*adj.* 可用的
suitable〔'sutəb!〕*adj.* 適合的　　chef〔ʃɛf〕*n.* 主厨
à la carte〔,ɑlə'kɑrt〕*adj.*(照菜單上各菜之定價) 點菜的
sparerib〔'spɛr,rɪb〕*n.* 排骨肉
reduce〔rɪ'djus〕*v.*減少　　serve〔sɝv〕*v.* 上 (菜)

中國菜進餐時的服務

Service during
the Course of the Meal

Dialogue : *W* = **Waiter** 服務生　　*G* = **Guest** 客人

W : Your *Shark's Fin Soup*, sir. May I serve you ?
　　　您的魚翅湯來了。要我服務嗎？

G : Yes, please. 麻煩你了。

W : Please enjoy your soup. 請享用您的湯。

G : Thank you. 謝謝你。

＊＊＊＊＊＊＊＊＊＊＊＊＊＊＊＊＊＊＊＊＊＊＊＊＊＊＊

W : Your *Fried Shrimp Balls.* 您的炸蝦球。

G : Shrimp！ Are you sure there's shrimp inside？ *It sure doesn't look like it*！
　　　蝦子！你確定裡面有蝦子嗎？它看起來實在不像蝦子！

W : It's made from ground fresh shrimps, sir.
　　　先生，它是用磨碎的鮮蝦做成的。

G : Hm. By the way, what's this seasoning made from ?
　　　嗯。對了，這調味料是用什麼做的？

W : *It's a mixture of pepper and various spices*. It should be sprinkled on your food.

那是胡椒和多種香料混合成的，您應該把它灑在食物上。

G : I see. What do you call these?

我知道了。這些你們叫做什麼？

W : They are called *Chinese Dumplings*. Please mix a little soy sauce and sesame oil on this plate and *dip them into it before eating*.

這些叫做水餃，請加一點醬油和麻油在碟子上，吃前沾一下。

G : Right. Thanks a lot.

好的，非常謝謝你。

W : You're welcome, sir. Please enjoy your meal.

不客氣，先生。請好好享用。

活用例句精華

① The *Jasmine Tea* is complimentary, sir.

① 茉莉香片是免費的，先生。

② Would you like something else to drink?

② 您還要喝點別的嗎？

③ *Please wrap* the *Peking Duck in the pancake* with the spring onion and the sweet bean sauce.

③ 請將北平烤鴨、葱和甜麵醬包在薄煎餅裡面。

④ *This is the complete course*. There is dessert to follow.

④ 這是全部的菜，接下來有點心。

shark's fin　魚翅

shrimp〔ʃrɪmp〕*n.* 小蝦

inside〔'ɪn'saɪd〕*adv.* 在內部

ground〔graʊnd〕*adj.* 磨碎的

by the way "順便一提"

seasoning〔'sizn̩ɪŋ〕*n.* 調味料

mixture〔'mɪkstʃɚ〕*n.* 混合　　pepper〔'pɛpɚ〕*n.* 胡椒

various〔'vɛrɪəs〕*adj.* 多種的

spice〔spaɪs〕*n.* 香料　　　sprinkle〔'sprɪŋkl̩〕*v.* 灑

dumpling〔'dʌmplɪŋ〕*n.* 蒸或煮的麵糰

soy sauce 醬油　　mustard〔'mʌstəd〕*n.* 芥茉

dip〔dɪp〕*v.* 沾　　jasmine〔'dʒæsmɪn〕*n.* 茉莉

complimentary〔ˌkɑmplə'mɛntərɪ〕*adj.* 免費的

wrap〔ræp〕*v.* 包裝

pancake〔'pæn,kek〕*n.* 薄煎餅

onion〔'ʌnjən〕*n.* 洋葱

complete〔kəm'plit〕*adj.* 完整的

dessert〔dɪ'zɚt〕*n.* 餐後的甜點心

請把鹽瓶遞給我

如果鹽瓶、胡椒粉瓶、糖罐等不在你面前，切勿伸手到別人面前抓取，或站起來自己去拿，只要對身旁的人說 *"May I have the pepper?"* *"Please pass me the salt."* *"Hand me the sugar bowl, please."* 即可。如果鹽瓶等在隔鄰第三、四位客人面前，則旁邊的人會代你轉問，然後逐一傳遞給你。

此外，也可以直接向服務生要：

"May I have the creamer（ paper napkin holder ）?"*

　　請給我奶精罐（紙餐巾盒）好嗎？

"Can you bring me the catchup(mustard, hot sauce)?"*

　　請拿著蕃茄醬（芥末、辣椒醬）來好嗎？

千萬不可存著「不好意思打擾別人」的心理，自己動手拿反而使別人認為你沒有教養。

詢問餐廳營業時間
Restaurant Service Time

Dialogue : *C* = **Caller** 打電話詢問者 　　*W* = **Waiter** 服務生

C : Is that the Japanese Restaurant ?

是日本料理店嗎？

W : Speaking. May I help you?

是的。需要我效勞嗎？

C : *What kind of food do you serve*?

貴店提供什麼樣的料理呢？

W : We serve a great variety of popular Japanese dishes in set courses and à la carte, and also many meat dishes.

本店備有各色各樣和菜和點菜式的一般日本料理，以及許多肉類餐點。

C : I see. That sounds fine. *Until what time are you open*?

我知道了。聽起來很好。貴店開到什麼時候？

W : We are open until 10 but *our last order for dinner is at 9.30 p.m.*

本店開到十點，但是九點半以後就不再接受客人點菜。

C : Fine. We'll be there before then.

　　好。我們會在九點半以前到。

W : Thank you, sir. We look forward to welcoming you.

　　謝謝，先生。我們期待您的光臨。

活用例句精華

① Which kind of food would you prefer?

① 你喜歡哪一類的食物？

② *We don't serve "Sushi" here* but there is a "Sushi" restaurant on the Third Floor.

② 本店不賣壽司，但是三樓有一家賣壽司的餐廳。

③ Would you like *to sit in a "tatami" room* or at a table?

③ 您要榻榻米的房間還是坐餐桌？

④ Excuse me, sir, but could you *take off your shoes* before walking on the straw mats?

④ 對不起，先生，在蓆墊上走以前請脫鞋好嗎？

---

serve〔sɜv〕*v.* 供應

variety〔vəˈraɪətɪ〕*n.* 變化；種種

set course 全餐；和菜

à la carte〔ˌɑləˈkɑrt〕〔法文〕(照菜單上各菜之定價)點菜

look forward to "期待；期望"

raw〔rɔ〕*adj.* 生的；未煮過的

take off "脫下"　　straw〔strɔ〕*n.* 稻草

mat〔mæt〕*n.* 蓆；墊

解釋日本料理的菜單

Explaining
the Menu of Japanese Cuisine

Dialogue：*W* = **Waiter** 服務生　　*G* = **Guest** 客人

W：Good evening.……Are you ready to order, sir?

晚安。……先生，您要點什麼？

G：Yes. What kind of food is the *tempura*?

甜不辣是什麼樣的菜？

W：*It is fish, prawns and assorted vegetables **dipped in batter
and then deep fried until crisp**.* It's very popular with
both Japanese and foreign guests.

那是用魚、蝦和各種蔬菜沾麵糊，然後一直炸到變脆，很受日本
人和外國客人的喜愛。

G：Um. It sounds delicious. We'll have the *tempura* dinner
for two, please.

嗯。聽起來好像很美味可口。我們要兩份甜不辣晚餐。

W：The *tempura* dinner comes with *raw fish*. Will that be
fine?

甜不辣晚餐加生魚片，這樣好不好？

G : I see. Well, I'll take the raw fish but *my wife doesn't care for it*. Could she have something else instead?

　哦。嗯，我吃生魚片，但我太太不喜歡。她能吃點其他的東西來代替嗎？

W : Certainly, sir. I would recommend the *"Chawanmushi"*. It's an egg custard with chicken, shrimp and gingko nuts.

　當然可以，先生。我建議點「蒸雞蛋羹」。那是加雞肉、小蝦、杏仁蒸的蛋羹。

G : O.K. She'll try that. 好，她就試試看那個。

W : Certainly. Just a moment, please.

　好的。請稍待片刻。

活用例句精華

① *This is the price per person* (*per head*).

①這是一人份的價格。

② The hors d'oeuvre is seasonal vegetables and fish.

②開胃菜是應時的蔬菜、鮮魚。

③ If you would prefer a light meal, I would recommend the à la carte dishes.

③如果您喜歡清淡的食物，我建議您以點菜的方式。

④ *I'm afraid that "Sukiyaki" or "Shabu-Shabu" cannot be cooked at the same table*. Would you like to sit separately or order only one dish?

④日本火鍋或涮鍋恐怕不能同桌煮。你們要分開坐還是只點一種呢？

⑤ What would you like to drink?

⑥ We have beer, whisky, wine or Japanese saké.

⑦ I'm afraid we don't serve cocktails.

⑧ *This is a hot towel for your hands.*

⑨ *There is no charge for green tea.*

⑤ 您想喝點什麼？

⑥ 我們有啤酒、威士忌、葡萄酒、日本米酒。

⑦ 我們恐怕不供應雞尾酒。

⑧ 這是擦手的熱毛巾。

⑨ 綠茶免費供應。

prawn 〔 prɔn 〕 *n.* 對蝦

assorted 〔 ə'sɔrtɪd 〕 *adj.* 各色俱備的

vegetable 〔'vɛdʒətəbḷ〕 *n.* 蔬菜

batter 〔'bætɚ〕 *n.* 蛋、麪粉、牛奶等和成之糊狀物

crisp 〔 krɪsp 〕 *adj.* 脆的

delicious 〔dɪ'lɪʃəs〕 *adj.* 美味的

custard 〔'kʌstɚd〕 *n.* 牛奶蛋糕(混合雞蛋、牛奶、糖)

gingko 〔'gɪŋko〕 *n.* 銀杏

hors d'oeuvre〔ɔr'dʌv〕 *n.* (正菜之前)開胃食品

seasonal 〔'siznəl〕 *adj.* 季節的

saké〔'sɑkɪ〕*n.* 日本米酒　　cocktail〔'kɑk,tel〕*n.* 雞尾酒

日本菜進餐時的服務

Service during the Course of the Meal

Dialouge：*W* = **Waiter** 服務生　　*G* = **Guest** 客人

W：Your hors d'oeuvre, sir.

先生，您的開胃菜。

G：Thanks very much. *By the way*, what is this thing under the chopsticks?

謝謝。順便一提，筷子下面這個東西是什麼？

W：*It is a chopstick rest*. We use it so that the tips of the chopsticks do not touch the table.

那是筷架。我們設置筷架，這樣筷子尖才不會碰到桌面。

G：I see. *Where can I buy a set*?

嗯，我在哪裏可以買一副呢？

W：There is a ceramic shop in the Arcade. They can also be bought at any glassware or china shop.

商店街中有一家陶器店。也可以在任何一家玻璃器皿或磁器店中買到。

G：*They will certainly make good presents to take back home*. 帶回家一定是很好的禮物。

W : Yes. They are very popular with our overseas guests. Please enjoy your meal.

是的。很受外國客人的歡迎。請慢用。

活用例句精華

① Please put a little of this horse-radish in the soy sauce, mix it well and then *dip the raw fish in it before eating.*

① 請把一些山葵放在醬油裏，攪拌好，在吃生魚片以前沾一點。

② Shall I bring you a spoon or a fork ?

② 要我替您拿湯匙或叉子來嗎？

③ *Please press this button for service.*

③ 需要服務時，請按這個鈕。

④ Please drink the soup directly from the bowl.

④ 請直接就著碗喝湯。

⑤ It's very hot but is more delic-ious *if allowed to cool slightly* before drinking.

⑤ 這很燙，但如果能在喝前稍微冷卻一下會更美味。

⑥ Please separate the chopsticks. *Rest them between the thumb and the forefinger.* Place the thumb on the left chopstick about a third of the way down. Rest the right chopstick on the ring fin-ger. Manipulate the chopsticks with the middle finger and the forefinger. *Only the chopstick on the left should move.*

⑥ 請把筷子分開，夾在大拇指和食指中間。把大拇指放在左邊筷子三分之一以下的地方。把右邊的筷子靠在無名指上。用中指及食指操作筷子。只要動左邊的筷子就好。

⑦ Please hold (*use*) them like this.

⑦ 請像這樣握住(使用)這個。

⑧ This is made with ground fresh shrimps mixed with......and steamed.

⑧ 這是用磨碎的鮮蝦拌上……蒸成的。

⑨ *It's made of ground fresh fish,* which becomes hard after steaming.

⑨ 這是用磨碎的鮮魚製成的，蒸過後會變硬。

⑩ *We can substitute a different dish* but I'm afraid there will be an extra charge.

⑩ 我們可以換另外一道菜，但恐怕需要額外的費用。

⑪ This is a dish for four persons.

⑪ 這道菜是四人份的。

⑫ *This leaf is for decoration only.* It is not edible.

⑫ 這葉子只用來做裝飾，不能吃。

⑬ I'm afraid that these dishes are not for sale. You may buy some similar ones at the ceramic shop in the Arcade.

⑬ 這些碟子恐怕不能賣。您可以在商店街的陶器店裏買到類似的東西。

---

hors d'oeuvre〔ɔr'dʌv〕〔法〕正菜前所上之開胃食品
chopsticks〔'tʃɑp,stɪks〕*n.* 筷子
ceramic〔sə'ræmɪk〕*n.* 陶器
arcade〔ɑr'ked〕*n.* 有拱廊的商店街
glassware〔'glæs,wɛr〕*n.* 玻璃器皿
horseradish〔'hɔrs,rædɪʃ〕*n.* 山葵
manipulate〔mə'nɪpjə,let〕*v.* 操縱；操作
decoration〔,dɛkə'reʃən〕*n.* 裝飾
edible〔'ɛdəbļ〕*adj.* 可食用的

甜不辣櫃檯的服務

Service at the Tempura Counter

Dialogue：*W* = **Waiter** 服務生　　*G* = **Guest** 客人

W：Good evening. A table for two, sir?

晚安。先生，兩位嗎？

G：Yes, please. 是的。

W：Would you prefer to sit at a table or at the counter?

你們喜歡坐餐桌或櫃枱？

G：We'll sit at the counter. *We'd like to watch the food being prepared.*

我們要坐櫃枱旁邊。我們想看食物烹調的過程。

W：Certainly, sir. This way, please. Please take a seat.………

好的，先生。這邊走。請坐………

Here is the dinner menu. …*We have set courses and also à la carte dishes.* Which would you prefer?

這是菜單。我們備有全餐，也可以用點菜的。你們喜歡哪一樣？

G：*We'll take the "A" course.*

我們要A餐。

W : Certainly, sir. Just a moment, please.

好的，先生。請稍等。

．．．

W : This is the sauce for the tempura. *Please mix the grated radish with the sauce* and then dip the tempura in it *before eating.* ．．．．．．．．．．．．．．．．．．．．．．．．．．

這是吃甜不辣用的醬。請把碎蘿蔔和醬拌在一起，在吃甜不辣之前沾一下。

This is the complete course. If you would like any additional dishes, please call me.

這是全部的菜。如果您還想要額外的菜，請叫我。

G : Fine, but I think this will be enough.

好，但我想這點就夠了。

W : *There is dessert to follow.* Please enjoy your meal.

等一下還有甜點。請慢用。

活用例句精華

① It may **be sprinkled with** lemon and salt.

① 這可能撒了檸檬和鹽。

② Would you like me to bring some ginger?

② 您希望我拿些薑來嗎?

③ **May I bring your rice now?**

③ 我現在可以端飯來嗎?

④ Would you like your rice now or later?

④ 您要現在端飯來，還是等一下?

à la carte〔͵ɑləˋkɑrt〕*n*. 點菜
grate〔gret〕*v*. 磨碎   radish〔ˋrædɪʃ〕*n*.紅蘿蔔
dessert〔dɪˋzɝt〕*n*. 餐後的甜點心
sprinkle〔ˋsprɪŋkḷ〕*v*. 撒；灑
ginger〔ˋdʒɪndʒɚ〕*n*. 薑

鐵板燒餐廳的電話預約

Taking a Telephone Reservation

Dialogue： *G* = **Guest** 客人　　*W* = **Waiter** 服務生

G： Hello. Is that the Sunny Garden Barbecue？
喂，請問是順利園鐵板燒餐廳嗎？

W： *Speaking*. May I help you？
是的，能為您效勞嗎？

G： I'd like some information about your menu. *What kind of food do you serve*？
我想要些有關菜單的資料。你們提供什麼菜式？

W： We serve many grilled meat, prawn and vegetable dishes *which are prepared in front of the guest*. We have both set courses and an à la carte menu.
我們供應多種烤肉、對蝦及蔬菜，都在顧客面前烹調。我們有和菜及點菜式的菜單。

G： What is the price range for the set menu？
和菜的價格大約多少？

W： *From* NT$ 500 *per person*. 一人份台幣五佰元起。

G : I see. Are reservations necessary?

我明白了。需要事先預約嗎？

W : We would advise you to make a reservation as the restaurant is often full.

因為本餐廳常常客滿，我們建議您事先訂席。

G : We'll do that then. *I'd like a table for four*, please, for this evening.

那麼我們要預訂座位。我要四個人的席位，今天晚上的。

W : Thank you, sir. *At what time can we expect you*?

謝謝您，先生。您什麼時候來？

G : At eight. 八點。

W : Would you prefer seats at the counter or at a table?

你喜歡櫃枱或餐桌的座位？

G : Does the chef prepare the food at the table?

廚師在桌邊烹調食物嗎？

W : Yes, sir. 是的，先生。

G : Right. *We'll sit at a table then*.

好。那麼我們要坐餐桌。

W : Thank you, sir. A table for four at 8 o'clock tonight. May I have your name, please?

謝謝您先生。今晚八點，四個人的座位。請問您貴姓？

G : Yes, it's Bernus. 我姓伯納斯。

W : *We look forward to welcoming you and your party.*

我們等著招待您及您的夥伴。

G : See you at eight o'clock then. 那麼八點見。

W : Thank you, sir. Goodbye. 謝謝您，先生。再見。

活用例句精華

① I'm afraid all our tables are reserved, sir. Would you mind counter seats?

① 我想所有的桌位都被訂走了，先生。您介不介意坐櫃枱邊的座位呢？

② Our last order is at 9 p.m. *Could you arrive a little earlier than that*, please?

② 點菜最晚到九點為止，請早一點來好嗎？

③ We close at 9.30 p.m. Could you come before that *so as to enjoy a leisurely meal*?

③ 我們晚上九點半關門。您能不能九點半以前來呢？這樣才能悠悠閒閒地用餐。

barbecue〔'bɑrbɪ,kju〕*n.* 烤肉
grill〔grɪl〕*v.* 烤　　　prawn〔prɔn〕*n.* 對蝦
in front of "在…前面"
look forward to "期待"
leisurely〔'liʒəlɪ〕*adv.* 悠閒地；不匆忙地

推薦鐵板燒的菜式

Recommending the Meal

Dialogue : *W* = **Waiter** 服務生　　*G* = **Guest** 客人

(After showing two guests to their counter seats)
（帶兩位客人到櫃枱邊的座位去之後）

W : Good evening. May I take your order ?
晚安。要點什麼菜？

G : The "B" course looks good but *what kind of portions do you serve*?
B餐似乎不壞，但是你們供應哪幾種菜式呢？

W : Would you prefer a light or a filling meal ?
你們喜歡份量少或份量多的食物呢？

G : We're rather hungry so it'll have to be *substantial*.
我們很餓，所以必須很豐富的。

W : I would recommend the "A" course then, sir.
先生，那麼我建議你們用A餐。

G : O.K. *We'll take the "A" course for two*.
好的。我們要兩份A餐。

W：The "A" course for two. Would you like anything to drink?
　　　兩份A餐，您要不要叫飲料？

G：Yes, some beer, please. 請拿啤酒來。

W：We serve only small bottles. ***How many would you like***?
　　　我們只供應小瓶的。你們要多少瓶。

G：***Make it two.*** 兩瓶

W：Thank you, sir. Just a moment, please. 謝謝，先生。請稍後。

活用例句精華

① Would you mind a seat at the counter？

① 您介不介意坐櫃枱旁邊？

② The "A" course comes with rice or chilled noodles. Which would you prefer？

② A餐附有飯或涼麵條，您要哪一種？

③ Would you prefer French or Thousand Island dressing？

③ 您喜歡法式或千島佐料？

portion〔'porʃən〕n. 一分（飯菜）
substantial〔səb'stænʃəl〕adj. 豐富的
chilled〔tʃɪld〕adj. 冷凍的
noodle〔'nudḷ〕n.（通常用複數）麵條

主廚和顧客間的對話
Conversation between
the Chef and the Guest

Dialogue: *C* = **Chef** 主廚　　*G* = **Guest** 客人

C : Good evening, sir. Your Lobster and King Salmon.
先生，晚安。您的龍蝦及特大號鮭魚。

G : That looks good. 那個看起來很棒。

C : Would you prefer Mixed Sauce or Japanese dressing ?
您喜歡什錦醬還是日本式佐料 ?

G : What's in the Japanese dressing?
日本式佐料裡有什麼東西 ?

C : *It's made of lime juice, vinegar and Soy Sauce*. It has
a very *subtle* and *refreshing* taste.
那是用萊姆果汁、醋和醬油做成的。味道清淡而且新鮮。

G : I'll try it then. 那我就試試看這個。

C : It *goes* very well *with* seafood or fish. How is it ?
這種佐料配海鮮或魚很好。怎麼樣 ?

G : It's delicious. *A very unusual taste*.
很好吃。味道非常特別。

C : Thank you, sir. …… 先生，謝謝。……

How would you like your steak？
您的牛排要幾分熟？

G : Medium rare, please. 三四分熟。

C : Certainly, sir. …… 好的，先生。……
Is this about right？ 這樣子可以嗎？

G : I'd like it done a little more.
我喜歡再熟一點。

C : Certainly, sir. …… 好的，先生。……
Will this be fine？ 這樣好嗎？

G : That's just right. *It looks very appetizing.*
這樣剛好。看起來非常開胃。

C : Please try the Garlic Sauce with it.
請加一點蒜汁嚐嚐看。

．．

C : There are fresh strawberries for dessert. Please enjoy
your meal.
還有新鮮的草莓當點心。請慢用。

G : I will, thanks. 我會的，謝謝。

活用例句精華

① May I tie on your bib？   ① 我可以替您繫上圍兜嗎？

② Will there be anything else？   ② 還要其他東西嗎？

③ *Would you like some more*……？   ③ 您要不要再來一點……？

chef〔ʃɛf〕*n.* 主厨；厨師

lobster〔'lɑbstɚ〕*n.* 龍蝦

salmon〔'sæmən〕*n.* 鮭魚

sauce〔sɔs〕*n.* 調味汁；醬

lime juice 柚汁；萊姆果汁

vinegar〔'vɪnɪgɚ〕*n.* 醋

subtle〔'sʌtl〕*adj.* 精緻的；淡的

soy〔sɔɪ〕*n.* 醬油   *go with* "配合；調合"

rare〔rɛr〕*adj.* 未完全煮熟的

appetizing〔'æpə,taɪzɪŋ〕*adj.* 開胃的

garlic〔'gɑrlɪk〕*n.* 蒜

strawberry〔'strɔ,bɛrɪ〕*n.* 草莓

bib〔bɪb〕*n.* 圍兜

6

用英文處理抱怨
Dealing with Complaints

如何應付客人的抱怨

　　在餐廳裏，難免會碰到客人抱怨（complain）的情形。有時是因為食物處理不善、口味不對勁、菜不新鮮等，有時是因為餐具破損、沒洗乾淨，這些事情往往引起客人將不滿的情緒發洩在服務生身上。雖然錯不在已，但服務生就是餐廳的代表，有義務提供客人完善週到的服務。

　　面對這些情形時，要記住「**顧客永遠是對的**」，委屈求全是生意興隆的第一步。除了少數存心找碴的情形例外，一般的抱怨必定是有原因的。因此，在處理過程中，要仔細聆聽客人的抱怨，並真心誠意地表示歉意。

　　如果是食物有問題，應立即更換，向客人說 " *I'll return your ～ to the Chef.* "（我把您點的～退回給主廚。）如果是餐具的問題，那麼馬上換一份新餐具就可以解決了。

　　萬一客人抱怨菜一直沒送上來，除了致歉外，**還要更積極地**表示 " *I'll check your order with the Chef.* " 然後催促廚房儘速送上。菜端上來時，不忘說聲抱歉 " *We're very sorry for the delay. Please enjoy your meal.* " 就能消解對方的氣憤了。

　　客人抱怨送錯菜時，則仔細核對點菜單，再將正確的菜式送上來。

對食物的抱怨及應對

Complaints about the Food

G. This steak is *underdone*!　　這份牛排火候不夠（未熟透）!

overdone	太老了
raw	半生不熟
bloody	還有血水
tough	嚼不爛
hard	太硬
dry	太乾澀

G. This soup is *cold*!　　這湯冷了!

lukewarm	微溫（不夠熱）
tepid	微溫
tasteless	味道太淡
flavorless	沒香味

G. This salad is *too oily*!　　這沙拉太油膩了!

not fresh	不新鮮

G. These eggs are *raw* !　　　　　　這些蛋沒煮熟！

　　　　　　too soft　　　　　　才半熟（沒煮熟）

　　　　　　too hard　　　　　　煮得太老

　　　　　　runny　　　　　　　沒煮熟

　　　　　　undercooked　　　　煮得不夠久

　　　　　　overcooked　　　　　煮得太久了

G. This food tastes *strange* !　　這道菜嚐起來味道很怪！

　　　　　　funny　　　　　　　　　　　不對勁

　　　　　　awful　　　　　　　　　　　很可怕

　　　　　　bad　　　　　　　　　　　　很差

G. This toast is *too dark* !　　　這土司烤太焦了！

　　　　　　too light　　　　　　烤得不夠

　　　　　　burnt　　　　　　　焦掉了

　　　　　　stale　　　　　　　不新鮮

　　　　　　soggy　　　　　　　沒烤熟

　　　　　　damp　　　　　　　濕濕的（沒烘透）

G. This ice cream is *soft* !　　　這冰淇淋太軟了！

　　　　　　melted　　　　　　　溶化了

　　　　　　runny　　　　　　　鬆鬆軟軟的

G. This tea is *cold* !　　　　　　茶是冷的！

　　　　　　tepid　　　　　　　微溫的

　　　　　　lukewarm　　　　　微溫的

　　　　　　too weak　　　　　太淡了

　　　　　　too strong　　　　太濃了

G. This juice is warm！　果汁是溫的！
This beer is flat！　啤酒走味了！

G. This wine tastes sour（vinegary）！
　　酒嚐起來是酸的（和醋一樣酸）！

G. This milk is off（sour）！
　　牛奶不新鮮（酸的）！

G. This butter is rancid！　奶油有腐臭味！

G. There's an insect in my salad！
　　我的沙拉裏有隻昆蟲！

G. There's a hair in my soup！　我的湯裏有一根頭髮！

活用例句精華

① I'm very sorry, sir. *I'll return your ~ to the Chef.*

② I'm very sorry, sir. I'll bring you some more.

③ I'm very sorry, sir. I'll bring you another one / bottle.

④ *Is there anything wrong with your order*, sir?

⑤ What would you like me to do?

⑥ There will be no charge for this. This is compliments of the manager. *This is on the house.*

① 非常對不起。我會把您點的～退回給主廚。

② 非常對不起，先生。我會幫您多取一些來。

③ 非常對不起，先生。我會替您送來另一份（瓶）。

④ 您點的菜那裏不對勁了，先生？

⑤ 您要我做些什麼？

⑥ 這不用付費。這是經理免費附贈的。這由公司請客。

---

tableware〔'tebḷ,wɛr〕*n.* 餐具
bloody〔'blʌdɪ〕*adj.* 血的
tough〔tʌf〕*adj.* 堅靭的
lukewarm〔'luk'wɔrm〕*adj.* 微溫的
tepid〔'tɛpɪd〕*adj.* 微溫的
stale〔stel〕*adj.* 不新鮮的
soggy〔'sɑgɪ〕*adj.* 沒烘透的
vinegary〔'vɪnɪgərɪ〕*adj.* 如醋的
rancid〔'rænsɪd〕*adj.* 腐臭的
insect〔'ɪnsɛkt〕*n.* 昆蟲
compliment〔'kɑmpləmənt〕*n.* 餽贈

對餐具的抱怨及應對

Complaints

about the Tableware

Dialogue : *G* = **Guest** 客人　　*W* = **Waiter** 服務生

G : *There's no ashtray on the table*！
　　桌上沒煙灰缸！

W : I'm very sorry, sir. I'll bring you one.
　　先生非常對不起，我會替您拿一個來。

G : *Could I have some matches*（*toothpicks*），please？
　　我能要些火柴（牙籤）嗎？

W : Certainly, sir. I'll bring you some.
　　當然，先生。我會替您拿些過來。

G. This glass is ***cracked***！　　　　玻璃杯有裂痕！

　　　　　　　　dirty　　　　　　　　是髒的

　　　　　　　　smeared　　　　　　被塗污了

　　　　　　　　spotted　　　　　　有污點

　　　　　　　　stained　　　　　　有污點

　　　　　　　　chipped　　　　　　有缺口

G. This knife is *blunt*！ 這把餐刀變鈍了！

                bent 彎掉了

           isn't *sharp* 不鋒利

        doesn't cut 切不下去

G. I dropped my fork on the floor.

我的叉子掉在地板上。

G. The food was dreadful. *I'd like a discount*.

這食物真可怕。我想要求打折。

G. The service was very bad. I'm certainly not paying the service charge.

服務很差勁。我一定不付服務費。

G. It's very noisy (*cold / freezing, hot / stifling, dark / gloomy*) in here.

這裏面好吵（冷/冰冷，熱/悶熱，暗/陰暗）。

G. Our table was in a very poor position.

我們這桌位置很差。

---

ashtray〔'æʃ,tre〕*n.* 烟灰缸　　toothpick〔'tuθ,pɪk〕*n.* 牙籤

cracked〔krækt〕*adj.* 破裂的

smear〔smɪr〕*v.* 弄污；弄髒

stained〔stend〕*adj.* 染污的；褪色的

chipped〔tʃɪpt〕*adj.* 有缺口的　　blunt〔blʌnt〕*adj.* 鈍的

discount〔'dɪskaʊnt〕*n.* 折扣；減價

stifling〔'staɪflɪŋ〕*adj.* 窒息的；悶熱的

gloomy〔'glumɪ〕*adj.* 陰暗的

對服務的抱怨及應對
Complaints about
the Wrong(Late) Order

Dialogue ❶ : The Wrong Order　*W* = Waiter 服務生　*G* = Guest 客人

G : Waiter. *This isn't what I ordered* !
　　服務生。這不是我點的菜！

W : I'm very sorry, sir. *What was your order* ?
　　眞對不起,先生。您點的是什麼?

G : I ordered a Shrimp Curry, not Beef Curry !
　　我點的是咖哩鮮蝦,不是咖哩牛肉!

W : I see, sir. I'll bring you some at once.
　　我明白了,先生。馬上給您送來。

（ *brings right dish* 送來對的菜式）

W : Your curry, sir. *I'm very sorry for the mistake*.
　　您的咖哩,先生。抱歉弄錯了。

G : Yes, please be more careful in the future !
　　嗯,今後可要當心點!

W : I will, sir. I hope you enjoy your meal.
　　我會的,先生。請慢用。

Dialogue ❷ : Complains about a Late Order

G = **Guest** 客人   W = **Waiter** 服務生

G : Waiter. *I ordered my meal at least thirty minutes ago* and it still hasn't come. Why is it taking so long?
服務生。我至少在三十分鐘前點的菜，到現在還沒來。為什麼要這麼久？

W : I'm very sorry, sir. *I'll check your order with the Chef.*
真對不起，先生。我會和主廚核對您點的菜。

G : Please do and hurry up！ I've got an appointment in fifteen.
minutes. 請快一點！十五分鐘後我有個約會。

W : Just a moment, please. 請稍等。

(*brings order* 上菜)

W : Your meal, sir. We're very sorry for the delay. Please enjoy your lunch.
先生，您的菜。抱歉耽擱了。請享用您的午餐。

---

shrimp〔ʃrɪmp〕*n.*（小）蝦
curry〔'kɝɪ〕*n.* 咖哩
careful〔'kɛrfəl〕*adj.* 小心的；謹慎的
at least "至少"   *hurry up* "趕快"
appointment〔ə'pɔɪntmənt〕*n.* 約會

當飲料灑在一般客人身上時
When Drinks Are Spilt
on a Guest

Dialogue： *G* = Guest 客人　　*W* = Waiter 服務生

　　　　　HW = Head Waiter（服務生的）領班

G： *Look what you've done*！　看看你做的好事！

W： I'm very sorry, sir. *I'll bring you a cloth immediately.*
　　　眞對不起，先生。我馬上拿布來。

G： Yes, and hurry up！　嗯，快點！

....

HW： Good evening, sir. I'm the Head Waiter and I'd like to
　　　apologize for our carelessness. *May I clean it up for you*？
　　　晚安，先生。我是領班，我爲我們的粗心道歉。我可以替您淸
　　　理嗎？

G： No, I'll do it myself！　不用了，我自己來。

HW： Are you a hotel guest？　您是住在旅館的客人嗎？

G： No, and what's that got to do with it？
　　　不是，那有什麼關係呢？

HW：Here is my card, sir. Could you send us the cleaning bill
and *we will refund the cost to you*?
先生，這是我的名片。請把清理費用的帳單寄給我們，我們會
把錢退還給您，好嗎？

G：I should think so, too！我想也該如此！

HW：We are very sorry to *have caused you this trouble*.
很抱歉給您帶來這種麻煩。

G：Yes, and please be more careful in the future！
好罷。今後可要當心點！

HW：We will, sir. We are really very sorry.
先生，我們會的。我們眞地很抱歉。

G：That's O.K. 算啦。

活用例句精華

① We have arranged a room for you
where you can wait until your
clothes are dry-cleaned.

①我們已替您安排好一個
房間，您可以在那兒等
到衣服乾洗好爲止。

apologize〔əˈpɑləˌdʒaɪz〕v. 道歉
carelessness〔ˈkɛrlɪsnɪs〕n. 粗心
refund〔riˈfʌnd〕v. 償付
trouble〔ˈtrʌbl̩〕n. 麻煩　　arrange〔əˈrendʒ〕v.安排

當飲料灑在飯店客人身上時

When Drinks Are Spilt
on the Hotel Guest

Dialogue： *HW* = **Head Waiter**（服務生的）領班　　*G* = **Guest** 客人

HW：Are you a hotel guest？您是住在旅館的客人嗎？

　G：Yes，why？是的，有什麼事？

HW：*We will arrange for your suit to be cleaned at once.*
　　　Could you accompany me to your room and change clothes
　　　there？
　　　我們馬上安排將您的西裝拿去送洗。能不能陪我去您的房間
　　　換下衣服呢？

　G：All right．好吧。

HW：May I have your room number, please？
　　　請告訴我房間號碼好嗎？

　G：Yes，it's ＃1234．好的，1234號。

HW：*After you*，sir．We are very sorry to have caused you
　　　this trouble.
　　　先生，您先請。很抱歉，給您帶來這種麻煩。

G : Yes, *it's a real nuisance*. 沒錯，的確很討厭。

(*Head Waiter accompanies Guest to his Room*)
（領班陪客人到房間去）

HW : Could you change clothes, sir, and give me the wet ones
for cleaning？
先生，請換下衣服並把濕衣服給我送去清洗，好嗎？

G : O.K. *Hang on a minute*. 好的。等一下。

HW : Thank you, sir. May I have your name, please？
謝謝您，先生。請告訴我您貴姓好嗎？

G : Yes, it's Wilson. *How long will it take to get them
cleaned*？ I'll need my suit tomorrow.
好。我姓威爾森。要多久才能洗好？我明天要。

HW : We will deliver your suit by twelve noon tomorrow.
我們會在明天中午十二點前把西裝交給您。

G : *Could you get it done a little sooner*？
你們能不能早點送來呢？

HW : I'm afraid our laundry is closed now.
洗衣部現在恐怕已經關門了。

G : I see. Well, I'll just have to wait then.
知道了。嗯，那麼我只好等了。

HW : *We are very sorry for the inconvenience, sir.*
先生，抱歉為您帶來不便。

活用例句精華

① I'm very sorry for the (*my*) mistake (*clumsiness*).

① 我為(我的)錯誤(笨拙)道歉。

② I'm very sorry to *have spoilt* (*ruined*) *your evening*.

② 我很抱歉破壞(毀壞)您今晚的興致。

③ Until which date are you staying, sir? *When are you checking out*, sir?

③ 先生,您住到哪一天為止?先生,您何時結帳遷出?

④ What is your *schedule* for tomorrow, sir?

④ 先生,您明天有什麼計畫?

⑤ I'm afraid the laundry is closed now. We will *arrange* for your suit to be cleaned *first thing tomorrow* and will deliver it by noon.

⑤ 洗衣店現在恐怕已經關門了。我們明早第一件事就是安排把您的西裝拿去送洗,然後在中午以前送還。

⑥ I'm afraid we cannot arrange to *have it laundered by the time you check out*. Could you send us the cleaning bill and we will refund the cost to you?

⑥ 我們恐怕無法安排在您離開旅館前洗好。請把清理費用的帳單寄給我們,我們會把錢退還給您,好嗎?

---

accompany〔ə'kʌmpənɪ〕*v.* 陪;伴　nuisance〔'njusns〕*n.* 討厭的事
Hang on a minute = *Just a second* "等一下"
inconvenience〔,ɪnkən'vinjəns〕*n.* 不便
clumsiness〔'klʌmzɪnɪs〕*n.* 笨拙
schedule〔'skɛdʒʊl〕*n.* 時間表

咖啡常用英語

△通常咖啡是餐後才喝的，為免太早端出來而冷掉，服務生通常會問：

" *Do you want your coffee now or later*? "
您是現在就要咖啡呢，還是等一下？

回答就說：

" *Now, please. Make it weak* (*strong*). "
現在，請泡淡（濃）一點。

△餐畢要通知服務生上咖啡時，可以說：

" *Waiter, may I have my coffee now*? "
服務生，現在可以給我咖啡嗎？

△想續添咖啡時的說法是：

" *May I have another cup, please*? "
可以再給我一杯嗎？

△服務生看客人的杯子快空了，會走上前來詢問：

" *Would you like a refill*? "
再給您添一杯好嗎？

電話的應對技巧
Using the Telephone

利用電話訂餐位

　　在西方，比較高級的餐廳都必須事先以電話訂位，有的餐館則因爲生意太好，座無虛席，如果事先沒預約，很可能有向隅之憾。

　　預訂席位的標準對話如下：

　　" *I'd like to reserve a table for two, please.* "
　　（我想預訂兩個人的餐桌。）

　　" *A party for two? Your name, please?* "
　　（兩個人嗎？請問貴姓大名？）

要問明總共多少人用餐時，可以簡單地說 " *For how many persons, please?* " 要問對方準備何時用餐，就說 " *At what time can we expect you?* " 最後還得問明客人的連絡電話，以便確認預約或臨時有事可以通知對方。

　　如果客人是好幾天前預約的，爲了提醒客人，並且確定預約的情形是否有變更，最好能在前一天打電話確認一下 " *I'd like to confirm your reservation for tomorrow（tonight）.* " 當然首先得表明自己的身份，然後將預約的內容重覆一遍：" Your reservation is for a table for four at 7 p.m. Has there been any change? "。一切都確定完畢之後，別忘了說聲 " *We look forward to welcoming you.* " 以致歡迎之意。

電話訂位的應答技巧

Taking a Telephone Reservation

Dialogue : *C* = **Caller** 打電話詢問者　　*W* = **Waiter** 服務生

C : Hello. Is this the Lien An Restaurant?
　　喂，是聯安餐廳嗎?

W : Speaking. May I help you?
　　是的，需要我效勞嗎?

C : Yes, I'd like to reserve a table for tonight, please.
　　我想預訂今晚的席位。

W : Certainly, sir. *For how many persons*, please?
　　好的，請問共有幾位?

C : *A party of six.* 六位。

W : At what time can we expect you?
　　請問幾點光臨?

C : Oh, at 7:00 tonight. 噢，今晚七點鐘。

W : Would you like a table in the main restaurant or in a
　　private room, sir?
　　先生，請問你喜歡大廳的席位，還是房間的席位?

C : *In the main restaurant will be fine.*
　　大廳的席位就可以了。

W : Certainly, sir. A table for 6 at 7 tonight. May I have your name and telephone number, please?
　　好的，今晚七點鐘，六個人的餐桌。可以告訴我您的貴姓及電話號碼嗎？

C : Sure. It's Franks and my number is 585-7092.
　　當然可以。我姓法蘭克，電話號碼是 585-7092。

W : Thank you very much, Mr. Franks. My name is Wang and *we look forward to seeing you.*
　　法蘭克先生，非常謝謝您。敝姓王，我們非常期待您的光臨。

C : See you tonight. Goodbye. 晚上見。

W : Goodbye. 再見。

活用例句精華

① *We have a table for six available at 8*, sir.
　　①先生，八點我們有六人的席位。

② Your reservation is *confirmed* for tonight.
　　②您今晚的訂位已經確定了。

③ How many persons will there be in your party.
　　③您一行共有幾人？

④ *Where can we contact you,* sir?
　　④先生，我們在哪裡可以和您聯絡上？

⑤ Thank you for calling.

⑥ I'm afraid we do not take reservations for breakfast.

G.*What price do your set courses start at*?

⑦ We have set courses from NT$ ～.

G. Do you have a children's menu (*portions*)?

⑧ We have already prepared your meal *for the reserved number of 10 guests*, and we will have to charge you for that number.

⑤ 謝謝您打電話來。

⑥ 我們恐怕不受理早餐的預約。

G. 和菜的起價多少？

⑦ 我們有從台幣～元起的和菜。

G. 有適合小孩的菜嗎？

⑧ 我們已經為您準備好預定的菜餚。所以，必須請您付十人份的費用。

expect〔ɪkˈspɛkt〕*v.* 期待；希望
private〔ˈpraɪvɪt〕*adj.* 私人的
look forward to "期待"
available〔əˈveləbḷ〕*adj.* 可用的；方便的
confirm〔kənˈfɝm〕*v.* 確定；訂妥
contact〔ˈkɑntækt〕*v.* 聯絡
portion〔ˈpɔrʃən〕*n.* 一分（飯菜）

客滿拒絕訂位的應答

Refusing a Reservation

Dialogue : *C* = **Caller** 打電話詢問者　　*W* = **Waiter** 服務生

C : Hello, is that the Farmhouse ?　喂，請問是農莊西餐廳嗎？

W : Speaking. May I help you ?　是的，需要我效勞嗎？

C : Yes, I'd like a table for 8 tonight.
　　　我想預定今晚八點的席位。

W : Just a moment, sir. I'll check our reservation list.……
　　　先生，請稍候。我查一下訂席單。……
　　　Thank you for waiting, sir. I'm afraid *we are fully booked for tonight.* Would you like to *make a reservation* at another restaurant in the hotel ?

　　　勞您久等了，先生。今晚的席位恐怕已經訂滿了。您要不要訂本飯店另一家餐廳的席位。

C : Well, *where do you recommend*?
　　　嗯，你建議的是哪裏？

W : What kind of food would you prefer ?
　　　您比較喜歡哪一種食物？

C : Let's see. *Something unusual would be good*.
　　我想想看。東西特別一點就可以。

W : Jade Garden serves many Chinese specialties.
　　翠園供應特製的中國菜。

C : That sounds interesting. 聽起來很有趣。

W : *Shall I transfer your call*, sir? 先生，需要我為您轉過去嗎？

C : Do that, please！ 麻煩你。

W : Could you hold the line, please？ *I'll connect you*.
　　請不要掛斷電話好嗎？我幫您接通。

活用例句精華

① I'm afraid *we cannot transfer calls from the house phone*. Could you dial extension 2345 directly, please？

①內線電話恐怕無法轉線。請直接撥 2345 號分機好嗎？

② Could you dial 9 for the Operator？ *She will connect you*.

②請撥九號給接線生好嗎？她會為您接通。

---

book〔bʊk〕*v.* 預定　　*make a reservation* "預訂座位、房間等"
specialty〔'spɛʃəltɪ〕*n.* 特製品
transfer〔træns'fɝ〕*v.* 移轉
connect〔kə'nɛkt〕*v.* 接通
house phone 內線電話
extension〔ɪk'stɛnʃən〕*n.* 分機
operator〔'ɑpə,retɚ〕*n.* 接線生

確認訂位的應答技巧

Confirming a Reservation

Dialogue : *W* = Waiter 服務生　　*TO* = Telephone Operator 接線生
RG = Reserved Guest 訂位的客人

W : Is that Industry Bristol, please?
請問是必治妥製藥公司嗎?

TO : Speaking. May I help you?
是的,需要我效勞嗎?

W : *May I speak to Mr. Marcus of the Sales Department,*
please?
可不可以請銷售部的馬克斯先生聽電話?

TO : Certainly, sir. I'll connect you.·········
當然可以,先生。我替您接通。·········

RG : Marcus, speaking. What can I do for you?
我是馬克斯,需要我效勞嗎?

W : Good morning. *This is Steve of the Hilton Hotel, La*
Pizzeria Restaurant speaking.
早安,我是希爾頓飯店義大利餐廳的史廸夫。

RG : Oh, hello. How are you today? 哦,你好嗎?

W : Fine, thank you. I'd like to confirm your reservation for tomorrow, sir.

　　我很好，謝謝。先生，我想確認您明天的訂位。

RG : Yes. 好的

W : Your reservation is for a table for four at 8 p.m. *Has there been any change*?

　　您訂一桌明晚八點的四人席。有任何變更嗎？

RG : I'm glad you called. *The number of persons is the same* but I'd like to change the time to 8:30 p.m.

　　很高興你打電話來，人數不變，但我想把時間改到八點半。

W : Certainly, sir. A table for four at 8:30 p.m. *We look forward to welcoming you*.

　　好的，先生。一桌明晚八點半的四人席。

RW : Thank you. Goodbye. 謝謝你。再見。

W : Goodbye. 再見。

活用例句精華

① You have ordered the NT$ 4,000 course for 6 persons. Has there been any change?

① 您訂了一桌台幣四千元六人份的酒席。請問有沒有任何變更？

industry〔'ɪndəstrɪ〕*n.* 工業
sales department 銷售部門
change〔tʃendʒ〕*v.* 變更；使改變

有外線電話尋人時的應對

　　有找客人的外線電話時，除了問清楚所要找的客人姓名之外，**還得詳細詢問客人的特徵**，這是因為一般餐廳不使用廣播設備找人，以避免吵擾到其他顧客。因此都是藉著拿 name board （名牌）或直接詢問的方式，通知客人接聽電話。

　　服務人員在接到電話時，務必請問對方客人姓名的拼法 *"How do you spell his name, please?"* 以便正確地寫在 name board 上。然後再請問客人有什麼特徵 *" Could you describe him, please?"* 當然，更不能忘記請教打電話來的人姓名，這樣才能提供客人初步的資料。最後，請對方稍等，不要掛斷電話，再請服務生去找人 " Could you hold the line, please? *I'll page him for you."*。

　　萬一實在找不到那位客人，要立刻拿起電話通知對方，不可拖延太久。這時，應該禮貌性地請問對方願不願意留話 *" Would you like to leave a message?"*。

客人有外線電話時
When There's a Telephone Call for the Guest

Dialogue：　*C*＝**Caller** 打電話查詢者　*W*＝**Waiter** 服務生　*G*＝**Guest** 客人

C : Hello. Is that the Coffee Shop ?
　　 喂，咖啡廳嗎？

W : Speaking. May I help you?
　　 是的，需要我效勞嗎？

C : Yes. I'd like to speak to Mr. Matthews, please. He should be in the restaurant having lunch *right now*.
　　 請找馬休茲先生聽電話。他現在應該在餐廳吃午飯。

W : *How do you spell his family name*, please?
　　 請問他的姓怎麼拼？

C : M. A. double T. H. E. W. S.
　　 M. A. 兩個 T. H. E. W. S.。

W : Thank you and *could you describe him*, please?
　　 謝謝，請描述一下他的外貌好嗎？

C : Yes, he's tall with dark curly hair and glasses.
好的。他很高，黑色捲髮，戴著眼鏡。

W : Could you *hold the line*, please? *I'll page him for you.*
請不要掛斷電話好嗎？我替您找他。

....

W : Excuse me, sir, but are you Mr. Matthews?
先生，抱歉。請問您是馬休玆先生嗎？

G : Yes, that's right. 是的，沒錯。

W : *I'm sorry to disturb you*, but there is a telephone call
for you.
很抱歉打擾您。有您的電話。

G : I see. *Where shall I take it*?
我要在哪兒接呢？

W : I'll show you the way. This way, please.
我為您帶路。請往這邊走。

---

page〔pedʒ〕*v*. 在公共場所呼喊名字以尋找(某人)
right now "現在；馬上"
double〔'dʌbḷ〕*adj*. 雙重的；加倍的
describe〔dɪ'skraɪb〕*v*. 描述；形容
curly〔'kɜlɪ〕*adj*. 捲曲的
hold the line "別掛斷電話"
disturb〔dɪ'stɜb〕*v*. 打擾；妨礙

替客人留話
Taking a Telephone Message

Dialogue : *W* = **Waiter** 服務生 *C* = **Caller** 打電話詢問的人

W : Thank you for waiting. I'm afraid *Mr. Matthews is not here at the moment*. Would he be in another restaurant ?
勞您久等了。馬休茲先生現在恐怕不在這裏。他會不會在別家餐廳？

C : No, he should be there. Could you *give him a message* when he arrives ?
不，他應該在那裏。他到的時候，請傳話給他好嗎？

W : Certainly, sir. *Go ahead*, please.
好的，先生。請說。

C : *I was due to have lunch with him* but I've been delayed. Could you tell him that I'll meet him in the Lobby at two ?
我本來要和他一起午餐，但是有事情耽誤了。請轉告他，我兩點在大廳和他見面。

W : May I have your name, please ? 請問您貴姓？

C : Yes, it's Johnson. 哦，我姓强生。

W : How do you spell that, please?
　　請問怎麼拼？

C : J.O.H.N.S.O.N.

W : ***Where can he contact you***, Mr. Johnson?
　　他可以在哪兒聯絡到您？

C : At my office. 在我辦公室。

W : May I have the number, please?
　　可以告訴我電話號碼嗎？

C : Sure, it's 234-8034. 當然可以, 234-8034。

W : Thank you. ***I'll give him your message***, Mr. Johnson.
　　謝謝。我會替您傳話給他，強生先生。

C : That's very kind of you. Thanks. 你真親切，謝謝。

W : You're welcome, sir. Goodbye. 不客氣，先生。再見。

活用例句精華

① ***Would you like to leave a message?***　① 您要留話嗎？

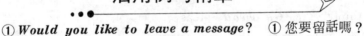

at the moment "此刻；現在"
give ~ a message "傳話給~"
go ahead 〔電話〕"請說話"
be due to "預定；準備"　delay 〔dɪ'le〕 v. 耽擱
lobby 〔'labɪ〕 n. 旅館（或戲院等的）大廳（休息室）
leave a message "留話"

6

傳話給客人

Giving the Message

Dialogue : *G* = **Guest** 客人　　*W* = **Waiter** 服務生

G : Waiter. *I'm expecting a friend* but he hasn't arrived.
Did he leave a message for me ?
服務生，我在等朋友但他還没到。他有留話給我嗎？

W : May I have your name, please?
請問您貴姓？

G : Yes, it's Matthews. 嗯，我姓馬休兹。

W : And may I have his name, please ?
請問您的朋友貴姓？

G : Yes, it's Johnson. 他姓强生。

W : Just a moment, sir. *I'll check for you.*
先生，請稍後。我查查看。

....

W： Excuse me, Mr. Matthews. Mr. Johnson called ten minutes ago and *asked you to meet him in the Lobby at two.* His number is 234-8034.

　　抱歉，馬休玆先生。強生先生十分鐘前打電話來過，他要您兩點在大廳與他碰面。他的電話是 234-8034。

G： I see. Thanks. 我知道了。謝謝。

W： You're welcome, sir. 不客氣，先生。

活用例句精華

① I'm afraid *no message has been left for you.*

① 恐怕没有人留話給您。

② Could you describe them, please?

② 請描述他們的外貌好嗎？

③ I'm afraid *they left about 10 minutes ago.*

③ 他們恐怕十分鐘前就離開了。

查詢營業時間時的應對

　　一般打到餐廳來的電話除了預約餐位和尋人之外，最常詢問的事項是營業時間、餐飲內容和尋找失物。

　　關於營業時間，不外乎是客人想知道餐廳幾時開門營業、幾時打烊，這時只需回答 " The restaurant opens at 11 a.m. and closes at 10 p.m. " 或是 " The restaurant's hours are from 11 a.m. until 10 p.m. " 。

　　如果是查詢有關餐廳的餐飲內容時，除了約略地告訴客人，我們供應四川菜、江浙菜、西餐或瑞士菜等，最好也介紹一下特別的拿手好菜（ specialty ），必要時得提供客人價格方面的資料。所以接聽電話的服務人員，手邊應隨時備有一份餐廳的英文菜單。客人詢問時，只要依照上面的資料回答即可。

　　如果是客人用餐後，將物品遺留在餐廳內，那麼要請他描述一下所遺失的物品特徵 " Could you describe them, please ? " 是否記得遺落何處 " Do you remember where you left it ? " 然後請他稍候，儘快去找。

　　如果找到了，可以請他過來取回失物 " We have found your ～。Would you come here and collect them? " 。萬一實在找不到，那麼只好告訴他 " I am afraid that they were not found in the restaurant. " 請他留下聯絡的電話或住址，以便找到時，可以立即通知他。

詢問餐廳的營業時間

Restaurant Service Time

G. *When does the restaurant open*? 餐廳幾點開始營業?

W. The restaurant opens at 11 a.m.
  餐廳早上十一點開始營業。

G. *When does the restaurant close*? 餐廳幾點打烊?

W. The restaurant closes at 10 p.m. 餐廳晚上十點打烊。

G. *When is the restaurant open for breakfast*?
  餐廳幾點開始供應早餐。

W. The restaurant is open for breakfast from 6 a.m.
  until 10 a.m. 餐廳從早上六點到十點供應早餐。

G. *What are the restaurant's hours*? 請問餐廳的營業時間?

W. The restaurant's hours are from 11 a.m. until
  10 p.m. 餐廳的營業時間從早上十一點到下午十點。

G. *When do you close*? 你們幾點打烊?

W. Our last order is at 10 p.m. Could you arrive
  before then, please?
  我們到十點停止接受點菜,請在十點以前光臨好嗎?

8

詢問遺失物品時

When a Guest
Calls about Lost Property

Dialogue : *G* = **Guest** 客人　　*W* = **Waiter** 服務生

G : Is that the Coffee Shop？ 請問是咖啡廳嗎？

W : Speaking. May I help you？ 是的，需要我效勞嗎？

G : Yes. I had breakfast in your restaurant this morning and
left my spectacles there. Have you found them？
我今天早上在貴餐廳用餐，而把眼鏡遺落在那邊。你們有沒有看
到？

W : May I have your name, please？ 請問您貴姓？

G : Yes, it's Talbot. 敝姓台伯。

W : Could you describe them, please？
請描述那副眼鏡的外形好嗎？

G : Yes, *they are a pair of brown ladies hornrimmed spectacles with blue tinted lenses.*
好的，那是一副棕色角質鏡框女用眼鏡，藍色鏡片。

W：Could you hold the line, please? I'll check for you.
請不要掛斷好嗎？我查查看。

....

W：I'm very sorry to have kept you waiting. We have found your spectacles, ma'am.
勞您久等了。我們找到您的眼鏡了，太太。

G：Wonderful. *Could you send them up to my room*?
太好了。請送來我房間好嗎？

W：I'm afraid we are very busy at the moment. Would it be possible for you to come here and collect them?
我們現在很忙，恐怕沒有時間。麻煩您過來拿好嗎？

G：O.K. I'll do that. 好的。我過去拿。

W：*Could you come to the Cashier's Desk at the entrance*?
請到入口處的出納櫃枱拿好嗎？

G：Fine. Thanks very much. 好的。非常謝謝你。

W：You're welcome, ma'am. 不客氣，太太。

活用例句精華

① Where were you sitting ?

　　① 您坐哪兒？

② Do you remember where you left it ?

　　② 您記不記得放在那兒？

③ *When will you be able to collect it* ?

　　③ 您什麼時候可以過來拿？

④ Could you come to the Coffee Shop now, sir ?

　　④ 先生，請現在就到咖啡廳來好嗎？

⑤ My name is An and *I am in charge of* ~.

　　⑤ 敝姓安，負責管理～。

⑥ Could you sign here, please ?

　　⑥ 請在這邊簽名，好嗎？

⑦ I'm afraid that they were not found in the restaurant. *Could you call the Lost and Found Department on extension 2157*, please ?

　　⑦ 它們恐怕不在本餐廳，請打到 2157 分機失物招領部好嗎？

⑧ We found your spectacles but *they have been taken to the Lost and Found Department*. Could you call them on extension 2157, please ?

　　⑧ 我們撿到您的眼鏡，但已送到失物招領部去了。請打電話到 2157 分機好嗎？

⑨ *They have been transferred to the Lost Property Section*. Could you come here in 15 minutes, please ?

　　⑨ 它們已經被轉到失物招領部去了。請在十五分鐘內過來這邊好嗎？

⑩ Where can we contact you in Taiwan?

⑩ 我們在台灣哪裏可以聯絡到您？

⑪ If we do find it (*them*) we will contact you immediately. *May I have your forwarding address*, please?

⑪ 如果我們找到，會立刻跟您聯絡。可以告訴我您的信件轉寄地址嗎？

property〔'prɑpətɪ〕*n.* 財產；所有物

spectacles〔'spɛktəklz〕*n.* 眼鏡

horn-rimmed〔'hɔrn'rɪmd〕*adj.* 邊緣用角質、龜甲做的

tint〔tɪnt〕*n.* 色彩　　lens〔lɛnz〕*n.* 透鏡

wonderful〔'wʌndəfəl〕*adj.* 極好的；絕妙的

cashier〔kæ'ʃɪr〕*n.* 出納員

in charge of "負責管理"

sign〔saɪn〕*v.* 簽名

extension〔ɪk'stɛnʃən〕*n.* (電話)分機

transfer〔træns'fɝ〕*v.* 轉移

forward〔'fɔrwəd〕*v.* 轉遞；轉寄

客人想借打越洋電話時
When a Guest Wishes to
Make an Overseas Call

Dialogue：　*G* = **Guest** 客人　　*C* = **Cashier** 出納員

G ：　*I'd like to make an overseas call*. Can I use this phone ?
　　　我想打越洋電話。可不可以用這隻電話呢 ?

C ：　I'm afraid overseas calls cannot be made from this phone.
　　　這隻電話恐怕不能打越洋電話。

G ：　Well, it's very urgent. I'm a staying guest, *can't you*
　　　make an exception for me ?
　　　嗯，這件事非常緊急。我是住在飯店裏的客人。不可以爲我破
　　　例一次嗎 ?

C ：　I'm afraid not, sir. *This phone is for business use only*.
　　　We ask our guests to use the guest room phones for over-
　　　seas calls. Could you make it from there, please ?
　　　恐怕不行，先生。這隻電話只能用於公事。我們請客人用客房
　　　的電話打越洋電話。請您從那裏打好嗎?

G ：　O.K. I'll do that, then. 好吧。那麼我就在那裏打。

C ：　I'm very sorry we couldn't help you, sir.
　　　非常抱歉不能爲您效勞，先生。

餐館活用例句

W: *How will that table in the corner do*?
　　牆角那個桌子好不好？

G: Don't you have a larger one? We have two more coming.
　　有沒有大一點的桌子？我們還有兩位要來。

W: *I'll pull two tables together. How's that*?
　　我把兩張桌子拼在一起，好嗎？

G: Juice comes with that order, doesn't it?
　　果汁不另外算錢，是不是？

W: *We charge you extra for it*.
　　要另外算錢。

G: I want a side order of Ham.
　　我要再來一份火腿。

G: *I'll skip the Mixed Fruits*.
　　我不要什錦水果了。

W: I'm sorry. Watermelon is *out of season*. How about canta-
　　loupes? 對不起，西瓜過時了，甜瓜怎麼樣？

W: We don't have them fresh, but we do have canned ones.
　　我們沒有新鮮的，但是有罐頭的。

W: *Please hold your napkin up*, the steak is hot and the grease
　　is splashing.
　　請把餐巾提起來擋一下，牛排很燙，油會四處濺。

G: *My steak is too rare*. Can you take it back and cook it
　　longer? 我的牛排太生了，請拿回去再烤久一點好嗎？

8

客房服務部的應對技巧
Room Service

客房服務部點菜方式

　　旅館中負責接受房客電話點菜，直接在房間內用餐的部門叫 Room Service（客房服務部）。Room Service 不但提供三餐的服務，同時全天候隨時供應各類點心。受理點菜的服務人員就叫做 Order Taker。

　　Order Taker 由於工作性質的關係，對各類餐點都必須十分熟悉，更必須知道餐廳服務生接受點菜時的英語應對。比如，房客預訂早餐時，得詳細問清楚是要煮蛋、炒蛋還是蛋捲 "*How would you like your eggs*, sir?"蛋裏要佐配火腿還是鹹肉 "*Would you like ham or bacon with your eggs*?"。

　　房客在打電話點菜以前，多半都已經看過房間事先備好的菜單，所以招呼之後即可請對方開始點菜 "Go ahead, please."邊聽電話邊將點菜內容記下來。這時，務必問清楚料理的方法和份量，諸如蛋要煮幾分熟，煎蛋是要 sunny-side up 還是 over-easy, over-hard, 牛排要幾分熟等等不可忽略的細節。

　　客人點菜完畢後，不忘說聲 "*I'll repeat your order.*"將點菜的內容覆述一遍。詢問客人什麼時候將菜送上去，乃至表明大約多久能送上去是非常重要的，這不但能給客人一份確定的感覺，更顯出服務人員的細心來。

前一晚受理早餐的預約

Taking an Order
the Previous Night

Dialogue：*OT* = **Order Taker** 受理點菜的服務生　　*G* = **Guest** 客人

OT : Good evening, Room Service. May I help you？
晚安，客房服務部。需要我效勞嗎？

G : Yes. I'd like to order breakfast for tomorrow morning.
我想點明天的早餐。

OT : Certainly, sir. Go ahead, please. 好的，先生。請說。

G : *I'd like two orders of fried eggs with bacon*, a large pot of coffee, two mixed salads, two orders of toast and some pineapple juice.
我要兩份煎蛋加醃肉，一大壺咖啡，兩份混合沙拉，兩份土司及一些鳳梨汁。

OT : *How would you like your eggs*, sir？
先生，您的蛋要怎麼煮？

G : Can you make one *sunny-side up* and the other *over-easy*, please？
可不可以一個煎單面，另一個煎雙面半熟呢？

OT : O.K. Which kind of salad dressing would you prefer, French or Thousand Island?
　　好的，您要哪一種沙拉佐料，法式還是千島？

　G : *Make them both with French dressing.*
　　都用法式佐料。

OT : How many orders of pineapple juice would you like, sir?
　　先生，請問您要幾客鳳梨汁。

　G : Two, please. 兩客。

OT : Will there be anything else, sir?
　　先生，還要不要其他的東西呢？

　G : No, that's all, thanks. 這樣就好了，謝謝。

OT : *I'll repeat your order.* Two orders of fried eggs, bacon, toast and pineapple juice. Two mixed salads and a large pot of coffee.
　　我覆述一次您點的菜。兩份煎蛋、醃肉、吐司及鳳梨汁。兩份混合沙拉，及一大壺咖啡。

　G : That's right. 沒錯。

OT : *At what time shall we serve breakfast*, sir?
　　先生，您要幾點用餐？

　G : Could you bring it around 8 o'clock, please?
　　大約八點送來好嗎？

OT : Certainly, sir. Have a good evening.
　　好的，先生。祝您有個愉快的夜晚。

　G : Thanks. You too. 謝謝。也祝你愉快。

salad〔'sæləd〕*n.* 沙拉

salad dressing 沙拉的佐料；生菜食品之調味汁

fried egg 煎蛋：

　　sunny‐side up 僅煎一面的荷包蛋

　　over‐easy 煎雙面半熟的雞蛋

　　over‐hard 煎雙面全熟的雞蛋

boiled egg 煮蛋：

　　soft boiled egg 半熟（約煮 2～2.5 分鐘）

　　medium boiled egg 七八分熟（約煮 3～3.5 分鐘）

　　hard boiled egg 全熟（約煮 5 分鐘以上）

omelet〔'ɑmlɪt〕*n.* 煎蛋捲（有乾酪蛋捲 cheese omelet、

　　醃肉蛋捲 bacon omelet 和火腿蛋捲 ham omelet）

poached egg 去殼水煮蛋（通常為 3～5 分鐘）

scrambled egg 炒蛋

egg in cocotte〔ko'kɑt〕蒸蛋

pineapple〔'paɪn,æpl̩〕*n.* 鳳梨

melon〔'mɛlən〕*n.* 甜瓜

watermelon〔'wɔtɚ,mɛlən〕*n.* 西瓜

papaya〔pə'pɑjə〕*n.* 木瓜

honey‐dew melon 哈密瓜

banana〔bə'nænə〕*n.* 香蕉

orange〔'ɔrɪndʒ〕*n.* 柳丁

coconut〔'kokənət〕*n.* 椰子

cherry〔'tʃɛrɪ〕*n.* 櫻桃

受理早餐點菜

Taking a Breakfast Order

Dialogue：*OT* = **Order Taker** 受理點菜的服務生　　*G* = **Guest** 客人

OT：Good morning, Room Service speaking. May I help you？
客房服務部，您早，需要我效勞嗎？

G：Yes. I'd like to order breakfast.
是的。我要點早餐。

OT：Certainly, sir. **Go ahead**, please.
好的，先生。**請說**。

G：Let's see. I'll have a fresh orange juice, a boiled egg and some toast and *marmalade*.
我想想看。我要一杯新鮮的柳橙汁，一個煮蛋，還要一些吐司加橘皮醬。

OT：*How many minutes would you like us to boil your egg, sir?*
先生，請問您的蛋要煮幾分鐘？

G：For three minutes, please.
煮三分鐘。

OT : Would you like ham or bacon with your egg?
　　您的蛋要加火腿還是醃肉？

　G : *Bacon and make it very crisp*, please.
　　加脆的醃肉。

OT : Would you like any tea or coffee, sir？
　　先生，您要茶或咖啡嗎？

　G : *Do you serve it by the pot or by the cup*？
　　你們是用壺還是杯子裝？

OT : By the pot, sir. 用壺裝，先生。

　G : Well, I'll have one pot of tea then, please.
　　　好吧，那麼我要一壺茶。

OT : With lemon or with milk？ 加檸檬還是牛奶？

　G : With milk, please. 加牛奶。

OT : Certainly, sir. Will there be anything else？
　　好的，先生。還要其他任何東西嗎？

　G : No, that's all, thanks. 不用了，這樣就好，謝謝。

OT : *I'll repeat your order*. One fresh orange juice, a three-
　　minute egg, very crisp bacon, toast and a pot of tea.
　　Will that be all, sir？
　　我覆述一次您點的早餐：一杯新鮮的柳橙汁、一個三分鐘熟的
　　蛋、脆的醃肉、吐司及一壺茶。先生，總共就這些，對不對？

　G : That's all. *How long will it take to arrive*？
　　就是這些。多久才能送到？

OT : Your order should take about twenty minutes, sir.
先生，您點的食物要二十分鐘左右。

G : Fine. I'll be waiting. 好的，我等二十分鐘。

OT : Thank you, sir. Have a nice day.
謝謝您，先生。祝您有美好的一天。

活用例句精華

G. *How many cups of tea are there per pot*?

G. 每壺茶有幾杯？

W. There are two cups of tea per pot, sir.

W. 先生，每壺有兩杯。

G. *How many slices of toast are there per round*?

G. 每份有幾片吐司？

W. There are three slices per round, sir.

W. 先生，每份有三片吐司。

G. *How many rashers of bacon are there per serving*?

G. 每客有幾片醃肉？

① Coffee for how many persons, please?

① 要幾人份的咖啡？

② We serve coffee in small or large pots. *The small pot contains two servings*, the large one contains four. Which would you prefer?

② 我們有大壺及小壺的咖啡。小壺的容量是兩杯，大壺的四杯。您要哪一種？

boil〔bɔɪl〕*v.* 煮

marmalade〔'mɑrml̩,ed〕*n.* 橘皮醬

ham〔hæm〕*n.* 火腿　　bacon〔'bekən〕*n.* 醃肉

crisp〔krɪsp〕*adj.* 脆的

pot〔pɑt〕*n.* 壺　　lemon〔'lɛmən〕*n.* 檸檬

repeat〔rɪ'pit〕*v.* 重複；覆述

per〔pɚ〕*prep.* 每

round〔raʊnd〕*n.* 圓而厚的一片麵包(loaf 的環切)

slice〔slaɪs〕*n.* 片

rasher〔'ræʃɚ〕*n.* 鹹肉薄片

serving〔'sɝvɪŋ〕*n.* 一份；一客

受理午餐點菜

Taking a Lunch Order

Dialogue : *OT* = **Order Taker** 受理點菜的服務生　　　*G* = **Guest** 客人

OT : Good afternoon, Room Service. May I help you ?
　　午安，客房服務部。需要我效勞嗎？

　G : *Could you send up some lunch*, please ?
　　請幫我送午餐過來好嗎？

OT : Certainly, sir. May I have your order please ?
　　好的，先生。請問您要點什麼菜？

　G : I'd like some Beef Curry and rice, a salad and some beer, please.
　　我要一些咖哩牛肉飯，一份沙拉和一些啤酒。

OT : Certainly, sir. *We serve a small salad with the Beef Curry.* Will you need a separate salad order ?
　　好的，先生。咖哩牛肉有附送一點沙拉。您還需要單獨叫一份嗎？

　G : No, you'd better *cancel the separate salad order* then.
　　不用了，那麼你最好把單獨叫的那份沙拉刪掉。

OT : Yes, sir. How many bottles of beer would you like ?
好的，先生。您要幾瓶啤酒。

G : How big are they ? 一瓶有多大？

OT : We only serve small half-pint bottles in Room Service,
sir. 客房服務部只供應小瓶半品脫裝的，先生。

G : Make that two then. 那麼送兩瓶過來。

OT : *Is there any particular brand you would prefer*?
您要什麼特別的牌子嗎？

G : I'll have Taiwan Beer. 我要台灣啤酒。

OT : How many glasses will you need, sir? 先生，您要幾個杯子？

G : Just one, thanks. 只要一個，謝謝。

OT : Certainly, sir. Will that be all? 好的，先生。這樣就好了嗎？

G : Oh, yes. *I've run out of cigarettes*. Could you bring me
some Marlboro, please?
哦，對了！我的香煙抽完了。請幫我帶一些萬寶路的香煙來好嗎？

OT : We don't sell cigarettes in Room Service, sir. *Could you
phone Housekeeping on extension 33*, please?
先生，客房服務部沒賣香煙。請打33號分機給客房管理部好嗎？

G : I'll do that then. 好的。

OT : Thank you, sir. Your order should be there in about 20
minutes. 謝謝您，先生。您點的菜將在二十分鐘內送到。

G : Fine, thanks a lot. Bye! 好的，多謝。再見。

OT : Goodbye, sir. Please enjoy your meal.
再見，先生。請好好享用您的午餐。

curry〔ˈkɝɪ〕*n.* 咖哩   cancel〔ˈkænsl̩〕*v.* 刪去；取消

pint〔paɪnt〕*n.* 品脫

particular〔pɚˈtɪkjələ〕*adj.* 特別的

brand〔brænd〕*n.* 商標；牌子

run out of "用完；耗盡"

cigarette〔ˌsɪgəˈrɛt〕*n.* 香煙

housekeeping〔ˈhaʊsˌkipɪŋ〕*n.* 管理；家政

Sea Foods 海鮮類：

carp〔kɑrp〕*n.* 鯉魚

cuttlefish〔ˈkʌtl̩ˌfɪʃ〕*n.* 烏賊；墨魚

eel〔il〕*n.* 鰻   halibut〔ˈhæləbət〕*n.* 大比目魚

herring〔ˈhɛrɪŋ〕*n.* 青魚；鯡

mackerel〔ˈmækərəl〕*n.* 青花魚；鯖

octopus〔ˈɑktəpəs〕*n.* 章魚

salmon〔ˈsæmən〕*n.* 鮭魚

sardine〔sɑrˈdin〕*n.* 沙丁魚

smelt〔smɛlt〕*n.* 一種鱗呈銀色之香魚

sole〔sol〕*n.* 鰈魚   trout〔traʊt〕*n.* 鱒魚

abalone〔ˌæbəˈloni〕*n.* 鮑魚

clam〔klæm〕*n.* 蛤；蚌   crab〔kræb〕*n.* 螃蟹

lobster〔ˈlɑbstɚ〕*n.* 龍蝦

oyster〔ˈɔɪstɚ〕*n.* 蠔；牡蠣

太忙時推薦其他餐廳

Recommending a Restaurant
When Room Service Is Busy

Dialogue : *OT* = **Order Taker** 受理點菜的服務生　　*G* = **Guest** 客人

OT : Room Service. May I help you ?
　　　客房服務部，需要我效勞嗎？

G : Yes, I'd like to order dinner. 我要點晚餐。

OT : Certainly, sir, but I'm afraid your order will take about
forty to fifty minutes to arrive.
　　　好的，先生。但是您的晚餐恐怕要大約四十到五十分鐘才能送
到。

G : Why so long ? 為什麼要這麼久？

OT : *Because this is our peak time for dinner orders.*
　　　因為現在是叫晚餐的顛峯時間。

G : Well, if it's going to take that long, maybe I'll eat
in a restaurant. *Where do you recommend* ?
　　　嗯，如果要那麼久，或許我可以在餐廳裏吃。你認為哪裡好
呢？

OT : Which kind of food would you prefer?

　　您比較喜歡哪一類食物?

　G : Something light. 清淡的食物。

OT : The La Brasserie serves *continental buffet dishes*, sir.

　　先生，巴賽麗之鄉供應歐式自助餐。

　G : Maybe I'll try there then. Where is it?

　　那麼，我可能會到那裏看看。在哪兒?

OT : *The La Brasserie is on the first floor of the Ritz Taipei Hotel.*

　　巴賽麗之鄉在亞都大飯店一樓。

　G : Fine, thanks a lot. 好的，多謝。

OT : You're welcome, sir. I'm sorry we couldn't help you. Goodbye.

　　不客氣，先生。抱歉無法為您效勞。再見。

活用例句精華

① I'd like something light (*filling, substantial, different*).

① 我喜歡清淡(份量多、豐富、與眾不同)的食物。

② The … *serves French Haute Cuisine* (*French Nouvelle Cuisine*).

② …供應法國名菜(新潮的法國菜)。

③ The … serves light lunches (*dinners*).

③ …供應清淡的午餐(晚餐)。

④ The … serves Chinese food.

④ …供應中國菜。

⑤ The … serves *steak* and *seafood dishes*.

⑤ …供應牛排及海鮮。

⑥ The … serves *Chinese buffet meals*.

⑥ …供應中式自助餐。

⑦ *We have a backlog of reservations* from last night. If you don't mind waiting, we will bring your order as soon as possible.

⑦ 我們從昨晚就積了一大堆預約。如果您不介意等的話,我們會儘快為您送去。

---

peak〔pik〕*adj*. 顛峯的;最高的
recommend〔,rɛkə'mɛnd〕*v.* 推薦;建議
light〔laɪt〕*adj*. 清淡的;易消化的
continental〔,kɑntə'nɛntḷ〕*adj*. 洲的;歐陸的
buffet dishes 自助餐
substantial〔səb'stænʃəl〕*adj*. 豐富的
cuisine〔kwɪ'zin〕*n*. 烹調;食品
haute cuisine〔,otkwi'zin〕*n*. 名菜佳餚;高級烹飪術
nouvelle〔nu'vɛl〕*adj*. 新潮的
backlog〔'bæk,lɔg〕*n*. 累積
as soon as possible "儘快"

甜點簡介

　　餐後吃點甜的東西，可以調節油膩。蛋糕、派、布丁、冰淇淋等餐後甜點（ *dessert* ）通常是晚餐的最後一道菜。大餐廳裏習慣上都是餐畢後再點。

　　餐畢刀叉斜放在餐盤右上方，刀双向內，此時服務生就會過來將不用的餐具全部拿走，使桌上煥然一新，只留下水杯、咖啡杯、鮮花、蠟燭及甜點的刀叉。然後再問客人：

　　・Are you ready for the dessert？

　　（現在可以點甜點了嗎？）

　　・What would you like for dessert？

　　（您要吃什麼甜點？）

　　可以隨自己的喜好點叫冰淇淋、蛋糕或各式的派。如果你還吃得下，則不妨叫一份蘋果派，上面加一球冰淇淋，這種 " *apple pie à La mode* " 頗能滿足老饕的口味。如果叫的是草莓蛋糕加冰淇淋，就叫做 " *strawberry cake à la mode* "。

　　美國的冰淇淋含脂肪較多，甜味較重。最有名的是Howard Johnson's 公司的二十八種口味（ 28 Flavors）冰淇淋，及Baskin -Robbins 公司的三十一種口味（ 31 Flavors）冰淇淋，式樣繁多。餐廳服務生通常會向客人強調這句話：

甜點簡介

" We have ice cream of all flavors. "
（各種口味的冰淇淋我們都有。）

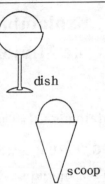

　　冰淇淋的容器叫 dish，所以常用 *a dish of ice cream* 做為計算單位，但是冰淇淋店零售外賣時則用 *a scoop of ice cream* （一杓冰淇淋）。

　　常見的聖代（ Sundae ）是指加有壓碎的堅果、水果、果汁、糖漿等的冰淇淋。例如巧克力聖代即是在一球巧克力冰淇淋上，淋一匙巧克力濃汁，擠上一團鮮奶油，灑上一把碎核桃及碎杏仁，再用紅櫻桃做點綴而成。

　　香蕉船的英文名字叫 *Banana Split* ，是將一根香蕉劈成兩半，平放在玻璃容器內，上面放三球不同口味的聖代，看起來像是一隻香蕉船。

　　Baked Alaska 有人譯成火燒冰淇淋，這是一種冰淇淋及果凍的組合物，上面覆以海綿蛋糕及一層厚厚的蛋白甜糕（ meringue ），食用前先放在烤箱中烤成黃褐色，也可以加上各種新鮮水果做為點綴。

　　Frozen Yogurt 稱為凍乳果，是一種由牛奶發酵製成的半固態食物，味道酸酸的，很受歡迎。據說餐後食用有助消化，最近頗有取代冰淇淋之勢。yogurt 也可拼成 yoghurt 或 yoghourt。

解釋最低消費額

Explaining
the Minimum Charge

Dialogue : *G* = **Guest** 客人　　*OT* = **Order Taker** 受理點菜的服務生

G : Hello, is that Room Service？喂，客房服務部嗎？

OT : Speaking. May I help you? 是的，需要我效勞嗎？

G : Yes, *could you send up a Coke*, please？
可不可以送一杯可樂上來？

OT : One Coca-Cola. Will there be anything else, sir？
一杯可口可樂。還要其他東西嗎？

G : No, that's all, thanks. 不用了，這樣就好。謝謝。

OT : Is this your first order from Room Service today, sir？
先生，這是您今天第一次向客房服務部點叫東西嗎？

G : Yes, that's right. 是的，沒錯。

OT : I'm afraid *the minimum charge for any first order is NT$70*. One Coca-Cola is NT$50 but we will have to charge NT$70 if only this is ordered. May we do that？
第一次點叫東西的最低消費額恐怕要台幣七十元才受理。可口可樂一杯五十元，但是如果只點這個，我們還是要收七十元，可以嗎？

G : Well, *make that a Coke and an order of waffles with maple syrup* then.

好吧，那麼來一杯可樂和一份雞蛋餅加楓蜜。

O T : One Coca-Cola and one order of waffles. Thank you, sir. We will send your order as soon as possible.

一杯可口可樂和一份雞蛋餅。謝謝，先生。我們會儘快為您送到。

活用例句精華

①There is a Coca-Cola vending machine on each floor near the elevator, sir.

①先生，每一樓的電梯附近都有一部可樂自動販賣機。

②Do you mind paying NT$ 70 for one order of Coca-Cola, sir?

②您介不介意付七十元叫一份可樂呢？

---

coke〔kok〕*n.*〔俚〕可口可樂（Coca Cola）
minimum〔'mɪnəməm〕*adj.* 最低的；最小的
waffle〔'wɔfḷ〕*n.* 雞蛋餅　　maple syrup 楓蜜
vending machine 自動販賣機
elevator〔'ɛlə,vetə〕*n.* 電梯

確認預約卡的方式

　　客人除了用電話向 Room Service 點叫餐飲之外，還可以利用 reservation card（預約卡）預訂早餐。只需填好房號、姓名、點叫的餐點數量、幾時用餐等資料，於十二點前將卡片掛在門把上，服務生就會來收取。Order Taker 拿到預約卡後，有任何疑問必須打電話向客人查問清楚。

　　打電話詢問時，首先說明身份、來意 *"We'd like to check your order"* 然後將問題一一弄清楚，例如：*" How many orders of tomato juice would you like?"* （您要幾份蕃茄汁），或是 *"Would you like toast or rolls with your breakfast, sir?"* （您早餐要吐司還是小圓麵包？）。

　　碰到預約卡上忘了註明用餐時間的情形時，表達方法如下："We received your reservation card, *but the service time was not marked.*"（我們昨晚收到您的預約卡，但上面沒有註明用餐時間），接著再請問對方 *"When may we serve your order?"* （何時將您點叫的東西送過去呢）。

　　在一般大飯店中，Room Service 都實行最低消費額制，Order Taker 必須主動向客人說明這項規定，*" The minimum charge for any first order is* NT$～"（第一次點叫東西的最低消費額是新台幣～元）。

早餐預約卡難以確認時

An Illegible Reservation Card

Dialogue ❶ : *OT =* **Order Taker** 受理點菜的服務生　　*G =* **Guest** 客人

O T : This is Room Service. May I speak to Mr. Gorton, please ?　這裡是客房服務部，可以請戈登先生聽電話嗎？

G : Gorton, speaking. What can I do for you ?
我就是。有什麼事？

O T : *We would like to check your breakfast order*, sir.
先生，我們想核對您早餐所點的菜。

G : Sure, what do you want to know ?
好的，你們想知道什麼？

O T : *Would you like toast or rolls with your breakfast*, sir?
先生，您早餐要吐司還是小圓麵包？

G : I'll have some rolls, please. 我要小圓麵包。

O T : There are three rolls *per portion*, sir. Will that be enough ?　先生，每份有三個小圓麵包。那樣夠嗎？

G : That's fine. 那就好了。

OT : How many orders of tomato juice would you like?
　　　您要幾份蕃茄汁？

G : Two, please. 兩份。

OT : Thank you, sir. *We will deliver your order at your re-quested time* (*at 8 a.m.*)
　　　先生，謝謝。我們會在您要求的時間（在八點）送過去。

G : I'd appreciate that. 我很感激。

---

illegible〔ɪˈlɛdʒəbḷ〕*adj.* 難以辨認的

deliver〔dɪˈlɪvɚ〕*v.* 遞送

request〔rɪˈkwɛst〕*v.* 要求

appreciate〔əˈpriʃɪ͵et〕*v.* 感激

roll〔rol〕*n.* 小圓麪包（cinnamon roll 肉桂小圓麪包）

whole wheat bread 全麥麪包

brown bread 黑麪包

buttered toast 牛油吐司

French fried toast 法式吐司

croissant Danish 可頌；牛角麪包

pancake 薄煎餅　　waffle〔ˈwɔfḷ〕*n.* 雞蛋餅

muffin〔ˈmʌfɪn〕*n.* 鬆餅

tomato〔təˈmeto〕*n.* 蕃茄

butter milk（提去奶油之）酸乳

skim milk 脫脂牛乳

yogurt〔ˈjogɚt〕*n.* 一種凝乳製品（如養樂多）

Dialogue ❷ : When the guest has forgotten to add the service time

O T : This is Room Service. May I speak to Mrs. Williams, please? 客房服務部。可以請威廉斯太太聽電話嗎?

 G : Speaking. 我就是。

O T : We received your reservation card last night, ma'am, but *the service time was not marked. At what time may we serve breakfast*?
太太,我們昨晚收到您的預約卡,但是沒有註明服務時間。請問我們幾點送早餐?

 G : As soon as possible. 儘快送來。

O T : Certainly, ma'am. Your order should be there in about 20 minutes. 好的,太太。您的早餐大約二十分鐘內送到。

 G : *I'll be waiting.* 我等著。

O T : Thank you, ma'am. Have a nice day.
謝謝,太太。祝您有愉快的一天。

沒有客人要點的菜時

When a Dish that the Guest

Orders Can't Be Made

Dialogue : *OT* = **Order Taker** 受理點菜的服務生　　*G* = **Guest** 客人

OT : Room Service. May I help you?

　　　　客房服務部，需要我效勞嗎？

　G : Yes, I'd like to order dinner. 我要點晚餐。

OT : Certainly, sir. Go ahead, please.

　　　　好的，先生。請說。

　G : I'll have a grilled steak, a green salad and *an order of French fries*.

　　　　我要一客烤牛排，一份生菜沙拉和一份薯條。

OT : I'm afraid *we cannot make any grilled dishes*, sir.
Would you like to try something else?

　　　　先生，我們恐怕不能做燒烤的菜。您要不要叫些別的東西？

活用例句精華

① *There is no grill in Room Service.*

② It is not *in season*.

③ It has been *sold out*.

④ It is not on the menu.

⑤ I'm afraid we cannot serve sandwiches yet, sir. *They are available from 11.00 a.m.*

⑥ I'm afraid soybean milk is only available until 11 a.m.

① 客房服務部不賣燒烤的食品。

② 這道菜不合時令。

③ 這道菜已經賣完了。

④ 菜單上沒有這道菜。

⑤ 先生，恐怕還無法供應三明治。三明治早上十一點才開始供應。

⑥ 豆漿恐怕只供應到上午十一點。

grill〔grɪl〕*v.* 烤；燒
French fries 薯條
in season "合時令"
sandwich〔'sændwɪtʃ〕*n.* 三明治
available〔ə'veləbḷ〕*adj.* 可用的；近便的
soybean milk 豆漿（亦作 soya milk）

客人想付現金時
When a Guest Wishes to Pay in Cash

Dialogue : *G* = **Guest** 客人　　*OT* = **Order Taker** 受理點菜的服務生

(*After the guest orders dinner* 顧客點叫晚餐之後)

G : Can I pay you *in cash* for my meal?
可以用現金付這份食物嗎？

OT : Certainly, sir. You may pay the Room Service waiter when he delivers your order.
當然可以，先生。您可以在客房服務生送菜時付給他。

G : *How much will it be*? 多少錢？

OT : Your dinner will be NT$875 including the tax and service charges. *Could you have the exact amount ready*, please?
您的晚餐是台幣八百七十五元，包括營業稅及服務費。您能不能把整數準備好呢？

G : Well, I'm afraid I only have a NT$ 1,000 note.
嗯，我恐怕只有一千元的鈔票。

OT : We will bring your change with your meal, sir.
先生，我們會將零錢隨晚餐一起送過去。

活用例句精華

① *We would like to bring your change when we deliver your meal*. Which denomination of bill will you be paying with?

② Yes, *you may use a meal voucher for Room Service* but if your order exceeds the value of the voucher, could you pay the difference, please?

① 我們很樂意將零錢隨食物一起送過去。您要用哪一種鈔票付款？

② 可以，您可以用餐券付錢給客房服務部，但是如果您點的菜超過餐券的總值時，請付差額好嗎？

---

pay ~ in cash "用現金付款"

charge 〔tʃɑrdʒ〕*n.* 費用

note 〔not〕*n.* 紙幣

change 〔tʃendʒ〕*n.* 零錢

denomination 〔dɪ͵nɑmə'neʃən〕*n.* (貨幣、長度、重量等之) 單位或類別

voucher 〔'vautʃɚ〕*n.* 收據　　exceed 〔ɪk'sid〕*v.* 超過

difference 〔'dɪfərəns〕*n.* 差額；差數

點叫飲料時的應對

　　飲料可分爲含酒精性飲料（ strong drink ），和不含酒精的飲料（ soft drink ）兩種。含酒精性飲料包括一切酒類，不含酒精的飲料就是一般的可樂、汽水、茶、咖啡等。

　　如果客人指明要某一種酒，如威士忌（ whiskey ）、白蘭地（ brandy ）、伏特加（ vodka ）等，則要問明想要哪一種牌子的酒 " Which brand would you prefer ？ "。有時客人還會要求 Order Taker 推薦，所以 Order Taker 必須兼具一些基本的酒類常識，知道什麼菜配什麼酒更能增添風味，並確定客人的喜好，最後才能大膽地說 " I recommend the ～ , sir "。

　　酒類有各種不同的瓶裝，客人可能不清楚，所以服務人員必須稍作解釋 " *We sell mini, quarter and half bottles, sir. Which would you prefer* ？ "（ 我們有迷你型、四分之一和半瓶裝，您要哪一種？ ）。最後問客人需要幾個杯子？ " How many glasses will you need, sir ？ " ，等一切都問明白之後，才可以掛斷電話。

　　不含酒精的飲料中，由於咖啡和茶有各種品牌，最好能請他從客房的菜單上挑選 " Could you choose one from the list, please ？ " 並問明需要的份量及杯子數目，因爲咖啡和茶通常都是裝在壺中送過去的。

客人點叫威士忌酒時

When a Guest Orders
Scotch

Dialogue：*OT* = **Order Taker** 受理點菜的服務生　　*G* = **Guest** 客人

OT： Room Service. May I help you？
　　　客房服務部，需要我效勞嗎？

G： Yes. *Could you send up some drinks*, please？
　　　可不可以送些飲料上來？

OT： Certainly, sir. What would you like？
　　　當然可以，請問您想喝什麼？

G： What is your House Scotch？
　　　貴飯店的招牌威士忌酒是什麼？

OT： It's Haig, sir.　海格牌。

G： Well, I'll take that then.　嗯，那麼我就點那個。

OT： *We sell mini, quarter and half bottles*, sir. Which would
　　　you prefer？
　　　　先生，我們有迷你型、四分之一和半瓶裝的，請問您要哪一種？

G： I'll take a half bottle.　我要半瓶裝的。

O T : We serve two bottles of mineral water, ice and *a plate of canapés* with the half bottle. Will that be fine?

　　　半瓶裝的酒我們附贈兩瓶礦泉水、冰塊和一盤餅乾。這樣好嗎？

　G : Yes, that's fine. 好的。

O T : *How many glasses will you need*, sir ?

　　　先生，請問您需要幾個玻璃杯？

　G : Could you bring two, please ? 請帶兩個上來好嗎？

O T : Certainly. We will send your order immediately.

　　　好的。我們馬上送過去。

活用例句精華

① *Which brand would you prefer* ?　　① 您喜歡哪一種牌子的？

② Would you like any *appetizers* with your drinks ?　　② 您要不要什麼開胃菜下酒？

③ How about some appetizers, sir ?　　③ 先生，要不要來些開胃菜？

Scotch〔skɑtʃ〕*n.* 蘇格蘭威士忌酒

mini〔'mɪnɪ〕*pref.* 迷你

quarter〔'kwɔrtɚ〕*n.* 四分之一

mineral〔'mɪnərəl〕*n.* 礦物

plate〔plet〕*n.* 盤子

canapé〔'kænəpɪ〕*n.* 加有菜餚、乾酪等之烤麪包或餅乾

　（常爲佐酒的開胃食品）

appetizer〔'æpə,taɪzɚ〕*n.* 開胃的食品

客人點叫葡萄酒時

When the Guest Orders Wine

Dialogue : *G* = **Guest** 客人　　*OT* = **Order Taker** 受理點菜的服務生

G : I'd like some wine with my meal.
我想點些葡萄酒佐餐。

OT : Certainly, sir. Could you choose one from the list,
please？ 好的，請從單子上選一種，好嗎？

G : I think I'll try a Chinese one. What are they like？
我想試試中國式的酒，它們是怎樣的酒？

OT : ***All the Chinese wines on the list are dry***, sir. Would
you like a red or a white wine？
先生，單子上所有中國式的酒都是無甜味的，請問您要紅葡萄
還是白葡萄酒？

G : A red would do. 紅葡萄酒好了。

OT : I recommend the Rosé, sir.
先生，我向您推薦玫瑰紅酒。

G : Fine, I'll have a half bottle of that, then.
好吧，那麼給我半瓶那種酒。

* *dry wine* 無甜味的酒

説明咖啡盤的使用方法

Explaining the Use of
the Coffee Server

Dialogue ❶: *G* = **Guest** 客人　　*OT* = **Order Taker** 受理點菜的服務生

G : Is that Room Service？ 請問是不是客房服務部？

OT : Speaking. May I help you? 是的，需要我效勞嗎？

G : Yes, I ordered a pot of coffee. It's arrived but *it seems
empty*. No coffee comes out when I pour.
我叫了一壺咖啡。已經送來了但好像是空的，我倒的時候沒有
咖啡出來。

OT : I see, sir. *Could you pull out the black stopper of the
pot before you pour*, please?
我知道了，先生。請您在倒以前先拉開咖啡壺的黑色塞子，好嗎？

G : Oh, is that what you do？ 哦，是這樣子的啊？

OT : I'll hold the line while you try it.
您試的時候，我暫時不掛斷電話。

G : That's very kind of you. 謝謝你的好意。

G： *It's working fine*. Thanks a lot.

　　我會使用了。眞謝謝你。

OT： You're welcome, sir. Please enjoy your coffee.

　　不客氣，先生。請享用您的咖啡。

Dialogue ❷：Explaining the Capacity of the Coffee Server

G： Is that Room Service？ 客房服務部嗎？

OT： Speaking. May I help you？ 是的，需要我效勞嗎？

G： *I'd like to make a complaint*. 我要跟你抱怨一件事。

OT： I'm very sorry to hear that, sir.

　　先生，很遺憾聽您這樣說。

G： Listen！ I ordered two pots of coffee but *the waiter only brought one*.

　　聽著！我叫了兩壺咖啡，但服務生只送了一壺過來。

OT： May I have your name and room number, please？

　　麻煩告訴我您貴姓和房間號碼好嗎？

G： Yes, it's Richards and I'm in Room ＃602.

　　嗯，我叫理查，住602號房。

OT： Just a moment, please. *I'll check our order list*.

　　請稍候，我查查點叫單。

⋯⋯⋯⋯⋯⋯⋯⋯⋯⋯⋯⋯⋯⋯⋯⋯⋯⋯⋯⋯⋯⋯⋯

Thank you for waiting, sir. I have checked your order.
We have put two orders of coffee in the one pot.

　　先生，勞您久等了。我查過您點的東西。我們把兩份咖啡裝在一個壺裏。

G : Oh, really. Sorry to have bothered you then.

哦，的確是的。抱歉麻煩你了。

OT : Not at all, sir. Please enjoy your meal.

沒關係。請慢用。

活用例句精華

① Your pot contains two orders of coffee.

② There are two orders of coffee in your pot.

① 您的壺裏裝了兩份咖啡。

② 你的壺裏有兩份咖啡。

server〔'sɜvɚ〕*n.* 盤；盆   pot〔pɑt〕*n.* 壺
empty〔'ɛmptɪ〕*adj.* 空的
pour〔por, pɔr〕*v.* 倒；灌
pull out " 拉開 "
stopper〔'stɑpɚ〕*n.* 塞子
capacity〔kə'pæsətɪ〕*n.* 容量
complaint〔kəm'plent〕*n.* 訴苦；抱怨
check〔tʃɛk〕*n.* 核對；查對   list〔lɪst〕*n.* 表
bother〔'bɑðɚ〕*v.* 煩擾
contain〔kən'ten〕*v.* 包含；容納

處理怨言的方式

　　客人打電話到 Room　Service 向 Order　Take 抱怨，通常都是因為點叫的東西遲遲不見送來。一般來說，客人向 Room Service 點叫餐飲有兩種方式，一是電話，二是預約卡（ reservation card ）。

　　預約卡在午夜十二點之後即停止受理。因此問明客人是用預約卡點叫東西時，應進一步詢問是何時將預約卡掛出來的 " At what time did you leave the card on the door?" 如果客人是午夜十二點以後才掛出來，那麼得客氣地向他解釋逾時不受理的情形 " I'm afraid that *reservation cards must be hung on the door by* 12:00 *midnight. We cannot accept orders placed after that time.*"

　　萬一是客房服務部的錯誤，要真心誠意地表示抱歉，除了向主廚查對之外，更要向客人保證很快就會把點叫的東西送上去 " You order will be with you very soon." 。

　　如果服務生將點叫的東西送到客房，而客人卻不在時，服務人員要把房號登記下來，隔一會兒再打電話上去，向客人說明這種情形，並詢問可否現在送上去 " When we delivered your order, you were not in your room. May we bring it now?" 這樣才不會招致客人不明不白的誤會。

抱怨所點的食物未送達時

Complaints about
Non-Delivery of an Order

Dialogue：*OT* ＝ **Order Taker** 受理點菜的服務生　　*G* ＝ **Guest** 客人

OT：Room Service, speaking. May I help you?

　　客房服務部。需要我效勞嗎？

G：Yes. I ordered breakfast from you last night for 8 a.m. but *it still hasn't arrived*!

　　是這樣的，我昨晚向你們點叫早上八點鐘的早餐，但到現在還沒送來！

OT：I'm very sorry, sir. Did you order by phone or by reservation card?

　　很抱歉，先生。您是用電話還是用預約卡點叫？

G：By reservation card. 用預約卡。

OT：I see, sir. *At what time did you leave the card on your door*?

　　我明白了。您什麼時候把預約卡掛在門上呢？

G：Well, I guess it was about 1 a.m. or so.

　　嗯，我想大約是凌晨一點鐘左右。

OT : I'm afraid that reservation cards must be hung on the door by 12 midnight. *We cannot accept orders placed after that time.*

很抱歉，預約卡必須在晚上十二點鐘以前掛在房門口。過了那個時間，我們就不受理點菜了。

G : O.K. Well, can you send up some breakfast as soon as possible? 好吧。那麼，你們能不能儘快送份早餐上來？

OT : It will take between 30 and 40 minutes at this time, sir.

現在可能得等個三、四十分鐘了，先生。

G : Well, *where can I get breakfast in a hurry*?

哦，我在哪裏可以很快地吃到早餐？

OT : The Coffee Shop and the restaurant serve breakfast at this time. 這個時間咖啡廳及餐廳都有早餐供應。

G : Maybe I'll try there then. 那麼我就去那兒試試看。

OT : *We're very sorry we couldn't help you*, sir.

很抱歉我們沒有幫上忙，先生。

G : That's O.K. 不要緊。

OT : Thank you, sir. Have a nice day.

謝謝您，先生。祝您有愉快的一天。

G : I will. 我會的。

---

complaint〔kəm'plent〕*n.* 抱怨；牢騷
delivery〔dɪ'lɪvərɪ〕*n.* 遞送
reservation〔,rɛzə'veʃən〕*n.* 預約
place〔ples〕*v.* 放置；定（貨）

抱怨送菜服務太慢時
Complaints about
a Late Order

Dialogue： *OT* = **Order Taker** 受理點菜的服務生　　*G* = **Guest** 客人

OT： Room Service speaking. May I help you？
　　這裏是客房服務部。需要我效勞嗎？

　G： Listen！ I ordered dinner about half-an-hour ago and *it still hasn't arrived*. Why is it taking so long？
　　聽著，我大約半小時之前點的晚餐至今還未送達。爲何拖這麼久？

OT： *We're very sorry for the delay*, sir. Could you hold the line, please？ *I'll check your order with the Chef*.
　　很抱歉耽擱了您，先生。請不要掛斷電話好嗎？我向主廚查查您點的食物。

....

OT： Thank you for waiting, sir. Could you wait a little longer, please？ *Your order is already on the way*.
　　先生，勞您久等了。能不能再稍等一會兒？您點的晚餐已經送去了。

　G： I should think so, too！ 我想也該送來了！

O T：We're very sorry to have kept you waiting, sir.
很抱歉讓您等這麼久。

活用例句精華

① Your order will be with you very soon.

① 您點的食物很快就會送到。

② Your order is ready now. We will send it up immediately.

② 您點的食物現在已經做好了，我們會立刻送上去。

---

delay〔dɪ'le〕*n.* 耽擱；延遲

I'll check your order with the Chef. 這是回答客人催菜時的公式化言辭。

on the way "在前往～途中"

immediately〔ɪ'midɪɪtlɪ〕*adv.* 立刻地

牛排的種類：

　chaliapin steak 夏里亞賓式牛排（牛排之一種，因夏里亞賓愛吃而得名）

　flank steak 腰窩肉牛排

　Hamburger steak 上好的肉

　minute steak 切得極薄的牛排

　rump steak 臀肉牛排

　round steak 大腿肉牛排

　sirloin steak 上等的腰肉牛排

　T-bone steak T骨牛排　　veal steak 小牛肉牛排

　tournedo 捲鹹醃肉的牛排

食物送達而客人不在房裡時

When a Guest Isn't in His Room
When the Order Is Delivered

Dialogue: *OT* = **Order Taker** 受理點菜的服務生　　*G* = **Guest** 客人

OT : Is that Room ＃639, please?
　　　請問是639號房嗎？

G : That's right. 是的。

OT : *May I speak to* Mr. Rendell, please?
　　　請找藍道爾先生聽電話好嗎？

G : Speaking. What can I do for you?
　　　我就是。有何貴幹？

OT : This is Room Service. When we delivered your order, you were not in your room. We have kept it here. *May we bring it now*?

　　　這裏是客房服務部。我們將您點的食物送達時，您不在房裏。
　　　這份食物還留在這兒，我們現在送去好嗎？

G : Oh, sure. 啊，當然好。

活用例句精華

① *I'm sorry to disturb you*, sir, but your order is ready. The waiter is bringing it now.

① 很抱歉打擾您，先生。您點的食物準備好了，服務生現在已經送去了。

各種調味品：

sugar〔ˈʃʊgɚ〕*n.* 糖

pepper〔ˈpɛpɚ〕*n.* 胡椒；辣椒

tomato catchup 蕃茄醬

mustard〔ˈmʌstɚd〕*n.* 芥末

vinegar〔ˈvɪnɪgɚ〕*n.* 醋

chilly sauce 辣椒醬

ginger〔ˈdʒɪndʒɚ〕*n.* 薑

garlic〔ˈgɑrlɪk〕*n.* 蒜

celery〔ˈsɛlərɪ〕*n.* 芹菜

olive oil 橄欖油

allspice〔ˈɔl,spaɪs〕*n.*（西印度所產之）甜胡椒

nutmeg〔ˈnʌtmɛg〕*n.* 荳蔻

clove〔klov〕*n.* 丁香

mint〔mɪnt〕*n.* 薄荷；薄荷糖

thyme〔taɪm〕*n.* 百里香；麝香草

tabasco〔təˈbæsko〕*n.* 辣醬油

anchovy sauce 鯷魚醬

chutney〔ˈtʃʌtnɪ〕*n.* 一種調味的果醬

cinnamon〔ˈsɪnəmən〕*n.* 肉桂

遞送餐點的服務

　　Room Service 的服務生在遞送餐點到客房以前，要先確定各種食器、調味料是否準備齊全，以免因遺漏而多跑一趟。

　　到了客房門口，敲門之後先打聲招呼，通報自己的身份 " This is Room Service. May I come in ？ " 得到客人的允許才能進入房間。

　　入門後，禮貌上要請問客人餐盤（或餐車）該放在哪裏 " Where shall I put the tray (wagon) ？ " 放好餐盤請客人簽帳時，可以說 " Could you sign here, please? " 在告退之前，最好提醒客人一聲「用餐後請將餐盤（車）放在門口走廊上」 " When you have finished, *could you leave the tray (wagon) in the hallway*? " 。

　　如果客人要給小費，可以表示 " That's very kind of you, but a service charge has already been added to your bill "。若客人要請你喝酒，可以職班時不准喝酒為理由婉拒 " I'm afraid we cannot drink on duty " 。

遞送食物
Delivery of Food

Dialogue : *W* = **Waiter** 服務生　　*G* = **Guest** 客人

W : Good morning. This is Room Service. May I come in ?
　　早安，這是客房服務部，我可以進去嗎？

G : Sure. 當然可以。

W : Here is your meal, sir. *Where shall I put the tray* (*wagon, trolley*)?
　　這是您的食物，先生。我該把餐盤（餐車、手推車）放在哪裡？

G : You can leave it over there. 就放在那邊。

W : *Could you sign here*, please ? 請在這裏簽個名好嗎？

G : I don't have a pen. Can I use yours ?
　　我沒有筆，能借用你的嗎？

W : Certainly, sir. Here you are.
　　當然可以，先生。請用。

　(*Guest signs bill* 客人在帳單上簽字)

W： Thank you, sir. When you have finished, *could you leave the tray in the hallway*, please？

謝謝您，先生。麻煩你用餐完畢後，將餐盤放在走廊上好嗎？

G： Yes, of course. 當然好。

W： Thank you, sir. Please enjoy your meal.

謝謝您，先生。請享用您的食物。

G： I will. It looks good. 我會的。它看起來很不錯。

活用例句精華

① *May I move these papers aside*, sir？

①先生，可不可以把這些文件移到旁邊？

② May I put these papers *on the writing desk*？

②可不可以把這些文件放在寫字枱上？

tray〔tre〕*n.* 盤；碟
wagon〔'wægən〕*n.* 餐車；送貨車
trolley〔'trɑlɪ〕*n.* 手推車
bill〔bɪl〕*n.* 帳單；發票；鈔票
hallway〔'hɔl,we〕*n.* 走廊
move〔muv〕*v.* 移置
aside〔ə'saɪd〕*adv.* 在旁地

服務顧客

Serving the Guest

Dialogue : *W* = **Waiter** 服務生　　*G* = **Guest** 客人

W : *May I serve your soup now* ?

　　我現可以侍候您用湯嗎？

G : Yes, please do. 好的，麻煩你。

W : Shall I open the wine now ? 現在打開酒瓶好嗎？

G : Sure. 當然好。

W : There is a warmer under the wagon. *Please help yourself but be careful* because it is hot.

　　餐車下方有個溫熱器，請自行取用，但是要小心，那東西很燙手。

G : Yes, I will. 好的，我會小心。

W : Could you choose two *French pastries*, please ?

　　請選兩種法式糕餅好嗎？

G : They look good. *By the way*, I forgot to order some coffee. Could you bring some up, please ?

　　看來很好吃的樣子。對了，我忘了叫點咖啡。請帶一些上來好嗎？

W : I can take your order, sir, but it will take some time.
*If you could give any additional orders to Room Service
on extension* #2, they can be delivered quickly.

先生，我可以受理您的點菜，但得花一點時間。如果您打 2 號分
機給客房服務部，另外再點叫食物的話，就可以很快送來。

G : I see, thanks. 知道了，謝謝。

W : You're welcome, sir. Please enjoy your meal.

不客氣，先生。請慢用。

活用例句精華

① I will place your order for you.
May I use your phone, sir?

① 我來替您點叫食物。可以
使用您的電話嗎，先生？

② That's very kind of you, sir, but I'm
afraid *we cannot drink on duty.*

② 先生，謝謝您的好意。但
很抱歉我們值班時不能喝酒。

③ That's very kind of you, sir, but
*a service charge has already been
added to your bill.*

③ 先生，謝謝您的好意，但
服務費已經加算到帳單裡
頭了。

---

warmer〔'wɔrmɚ〕n. 溫熱器
help oneself "自行取用"
pastry〔'pestrɪ〕n. 糕餅（以油、麵烤成的點心）
by the way "順便一提"
additional〔ə'dɪʃənl̩〕adj. 加添的；補充的
extension〔ɪk'stɛnʃən〕n. 分機
place〔ples〕v. 定（貨）；送出（訂單）
on duty "值班"　　charge〔tʃɑrdʒ〕n. 費用

客人要香煙時

When a Guest
Asks for a Cigarette

Dialogue：*G* = **Guest** 客人　　*W* = **Waitress** 女服務生

G：Waitress. Can you get me some cigarettes?
　　服務生，能不能拿些煙給我？

W：There is a vending machine *in front of* the cloakroom.
　　在存物處前面有一台自動販賣機。

G：Well, can't you get them for me?
　　嗯，能不能幫我買呢？

W：I'm afraid I'm not allowed to *leave my post*, sir.
　　我恐怕不准離開工作崗位。

G：O.K. I'll get them myself.
　　好吧！我自己去買。

W：*I'm sorry I couldn't help you*, sir.
　　我很抱歉沒幫上忙。

G：That's all right.
　　沒有關係。

活用例句精華

① I'm afraid the machine only stocks Lark and Chinese brands.

① 那機器恐怕只存有雲雀和中國的牌子。

② Mild or regular, sir?

② 淡味的或是一般長短的?

③ May I have NT$190 for the machine, sir?

③ 先生,請給我一百九十元投進販賣機好嗎?

waitress〔'wetrɪs〕*n.* 女侍者
vending machine "自動販賣機"
in front of "在…之前"
cloakroom〔'klok,rum〕*n.* 衣帽間;寄存物品之處
allow〔ə'lau〕*v.* 允許
post〔post〕*n.* 職位;工作

How to Use
Chopsticks
使用筷子的方法

外國客人通常很有興緻學習拿筷子的方法，這時你該如何用英文教他們呢？首先，你要強調學會控制手指輕輕移動筷子，得花點時間和耐心（*It will take a little time and patience to control light finger movements.*），而且手握筷子時只要花一點點力氣就夠了（*Chopsticks require very little strength or force.*）。再按照下列步驟慢慢地教。

A : The stationary stick is held with slight pressure between the second joint of the thumb and a half-curled fourth finger, just above the tip. The thumb is about two thirds from the end of the stick. Keep the chopstick ends even.

A：固定不動的那根筷子，輕輕地夾在拇指的第二指節處和半彎曲的無名指指端之間。拇指壓在筷子尖端以上三分之二處。同時保持筷子兩端平穩。

B : The moving or pinching
stick is held and positioned
between the thumb, and
fore and middle fingers are
bent inwards, thus bringing
the points of the chopsticks
closer together.

B：得移動來夾持食
物的那根筷子，握持
在拇指、食指和中指
之間的位置上。食指、
中指要向裏微彎。如
此輕輕地用力將兩根
筷子的尖端頂點靠近。

C : The chopsticks are held
loosely in a relaxed hand,
with the sticks slightly
apart. When a morsel is
desired, an inward bending
of the fore and middle
fingers will bring the two
points together. Ideally,
the chopsticks will meet
in a positive straight
movement.

C：握持筷子時，手
部肌肉放鬆，將筷子
微微叉開。要夾食物
時，食指和中指向裏
彎曲，筷子的尖端就
會靠攏。正確的握法，
筷子會俐落地依直線
前後移動。

新餐館英語

修　　編 / 劉宜芳

發 行 所 / 學習出版有限公司　　☎ (02) 2704-5525

郵撥帳號 / 0512727-2 學習出版社帳戶

登 記 證 / 局版台業 2179 號

印 刷 所 / 裕強彩色印刷有限公司

台北門市 / 台北市許昌街 10 號 2 F　　☎ (02) 2331-4060・2331-9209

台灣總經銷 / 紅螞蟻圖書有限公司　　☎ (02) 2795-3656

美國總經銷 / Evergreen Book Store　　☎ (818) 2813622

本公司網址　www.learnbook.com.tw

電子郵件　learnbook@learnbook.com.tw

售價：新台幣一百八十元正

2009 年 3 月 1 日新修訂

ISBN 957-519-078-5